Couldn't she be a different Marnie tonight—one who was seeking nothing but uncomplicated pleasure?

She had always been the responsible one. The one who looked out for other people—with one eye on the distance, preparing for the shadows that inevitably hovered there. Wasn't it time to articulate what *she* wanted for a change?

She cleared her throat. "Would you mind speaking in English so I can understand what you're saying?"

"Are we planning to do a lot of talking then, Marnie? Is that what turns you on?"

Something warned her she'd be straying into dangerous territory if she told him she didn't *know* what turned her on because she'd never given herself the chance to find out.

"*You* turn me on," she said boldly, and something about the breathless rush of her words made his powerful body tense.

"Oh, *do* I?" Leon questioned, tilting her chin with his fingers so that their darkened gazes clashed. "So what are we going to do about that, I wonder."

Sharon Kendrick once won a national writing competition by describing her ideal date: being flown to an exotic island by a gorgeous and powerful man. Little did she realize that she'd just wandered into her dream job! Today she writes for Harlequin, and her books feature often stubborn but always to-die-for heroes and the women who bring them to their knees. She believes that the best books are those you never want to end. Just like life...

Books by Sharon Kendrick

Harlequin Presents

Cinderella in the Sicilian's World
The Sheikh's Royal Announcement
Cinderella's Christmas Secret
One Night Before the Royal Wedding

Conveniently Wed!

His Contract Christmas Bride

The Legendary Argentinian Billionaires

Bought Bride for the Argentinian
The Argentinian's Baby of Scandal

Visit the Author Profile page
at Harlequin.com for more titles.

Sharon Kendrick

SECRETS OF CINDERELLA'S AWAKENING

ISBN-13: 978-1-335-56876-2

Secrets of Cinderella's Awakening

Copyright © 2021 by Sharon Kendrick

This edition published by arrangement with Harlequin Books S.A.

For questions and comments about the quality of this book,
please contact us at CustomerService@Harlequin.com.

Harlequin Enterprises ULC
22 Adelaide St. West, 40th Floor
Toronto, Ontario M5H 4E3, Canada
www.Harlequin.com

Printed in U.S.A.

SECRETS OF CINDERELLA'S AWAKENING

Big thanks must go to:

The lovely Emily, owner of Hair Jungle, Plymouth—for her insights on hairdressing.

And the fabulous criminal lawyer Janie Heard—for advising me on Pansy's fate.

CHAPTER ONE

IT HURT. It really hurt.

Marnie opened her mouth and yelled as she hadn't yelled in years. Crawling out of the water, she slumped onto the hard sand, shivering uncontrollably in her stupid orange bikini despite the heat from the late afternoon sun.

Just her luck.

Or maybe not. Unless she stupidly believed that fate wouldn't be cruel enough to throw anything else at her. Because since when had fate ever been *fair*? Fairness was what happened to other people. To people with homes and parents and food in their belly, and no reason to fear the creak on the landing.

Biting her lip, she tried to conquer the pain, which was coming at her from all directions. Because wasn't her twin sister in prison, grimly fulfilling the predictions made by so many foster parents all those years ago, while she was alone on a faraway Greek island, which suddenly felt more like a battlefield than the paradise she'd been promised?

Twisting her head, she surveyed her foot and a heel which was scarlet and speckled with black. She let out a whimper, barely noticing the shadow which was falling over her shivering flesh.

'What the hell has happened?'

The voice was deep. Authoritative. Marnie jerked her chin up to see the silhouette of a man blocking out the sun and she squinted. His torso was covered with droplets of water, which glittered like diamonds on his powerful frame, and he was out of breath—as if he'd been running. Rather distractingly his hand was positioned over his groin and she realised he was just zipping up a pair of faded jeans.

And despite her throbbing heel, Marnie felt a punch of vivid awareness because it was him. The swimmer. The man she'd noticed before she'd been bitten—if indeed she *had* been bitten—and not just because he'd been the only other person on the beach. Who wouldn't have noticed his wild, almost feral beauty when he'd arrived on a noisy old motor-bike and laid it down on the wide strip of sand?

With uncharacteristic fascination she had watched as he'd stripped off his jeans and T-shirt before running into the sea and diving beneath the sapphire froth of the waves. He had moved with a kind of elemental grace as he'd ploughed his way through the water—but his determined progress had looked more mechanical than joyful.

'Are you okay?' he probed, his rich voice edged with urgency. 'I heard you scream.'

Now her eyes had adjusted she could see him more clearly but despite his solicitous question, his face was hard, his mouth un-smiling. The sculpted contours of his features were unmoving, as if they had been ham-mered from some cold and unforgiving metal. Only his eyes looked alive as they raked over her and she wished she hadn't worn this bi-kini, which her workmates had given her be-fore she'd left London, more as a joke than because they actually thought she'd wear it. And if the elastic on her ancient one-piece hadn't finally snapped the flimsy garment wouldn't have made it out of the carrier bag. It was too tight, too small, too everything really and it was making her feel almost naked beneath the man's burning gaze.

Marnie shook her head, wet strands of hair flopping onto her shoulders. And because she was in pain and because he was making her feel something she wasn't used to feeling and didn't particularly like, she took refuge in sarcasm. 'Does it look like I'm okay?' she demanded.

He looked slightly surprised and then irritated, as if he weren't used to women talking to him that way. 'What have you done?'

'I don't *know*!' she wailed. 'It's my foot.'

'Let me see.'

She wanted to tell him to go away. She wanted to tell him she could take care of herself because that was always her default mechanism, but he was crouching down and cradling her foot in the palm of his hand, before running the edge of his thumb over the heel with what felt like consummate expertise. And that one simple act made Marnie's stomach turn to jelly.

She wasn't used to being handled by anyone, but especially not by a man. Parentless kids didn't get cuddled much in her experience—and when you did, you viewed it with suspicion and tried to avoid it wherever possible for there was usually some sort of agenda involved. That habit had carried over into adulthood and avoiding physical contact had made her life less complicated. Unlike her friends, she didn't have sex only to regret it afterwards, and she'd never suffered from unrequited love or a broken heart. She feared intimacy with the natural aversion of someone who had never come into contact with it and the only person she had ever loved had been her twin sister.

But the stranger's touch was having a potent effect on her—it was driving everything from her mind other than how *good* he was making her feel and the sensation took her by surprise because it felt irrational. It also felt like emotion—and Marnie didn't do *that* either. She'd taught herself not to care because you didn't get hurt if you didn't care.

'So what's happened? Have I been bitten by some deadly Greek sea serpent or something?' she questioned.

He lifted his head then and she almost wished he hadn't because his eyes were so blue that they made the sky behind him fade into insignificance.

'A sea urchin, actually,' he amended coolly. 'And they do have the potential to be dangerous. Certainly not something you can ignore, or be flippant about. I have something in my bike which can sort it out for you. Wait here.'

His response sounded halfway between a reprimand and an order and Marnie opened her mouth to tell him not to bother, but thought better of it and shut it again because really—what choice did she have?

'Suit yourself,' she said.

Leon scowled as he turned away, retracing his route across the beach towards his motorbike and wondering why the hell he had made the mistake of getting involved with such a fractious female. Afternoons off in his crazy busy life were rare and riding to the top of the island to watch the sunset had been his only plan for the rest of the day, before the whirl of the upcoming weekend descended on him.

It was strange being back in Greece. It always was. He'd been away for a long time and trips to his homeland had been erratic, for he had made his fortune in America and Europe. But there had been a couple of tentative meetings with his father over recent years, leading to an uneasy reconciliation after a long period of estrangement. Soon he would attend the wedding of the man who had sired him, telling himself it was the right thing to do, even if found the prospect distasteful. But his father was an old man now and who knew how long he had left?

With an effort, Leon pushed the thought away and regarded instead the weekend which lay ahead of him. His mouth relaxed by a fraction. He owed it to one of his oldest friends to put in an appearance for his birthday celebrations and at least he'd be able to enjoy some down time. At least, that was the theory. In truth he didn't really *do* relaxation, no matter how much he tried. He did adrenalin and hunger and drive. He worked better with projects than with people and nothing distracted him from his primary purpose— of remaining one of the most successful self-made men to ever come out of Greece. And that was important to him. It had been the main salvage to his pride and self-respect after the bitter chaos of the past.

His scowl deepened as he reached his bike and opened up one of the dusty panniers, because rescuing damsels in distress certainly hadn't been on his agenda, especially one who answered back as much as this one did. But despite the bitter accusations sometimes levelled at him by women who had tried and failed to pin him down, he wasn't *completely* devoid of conscience. What else could he do but help the stricken blonde, even if she seemed remarkably ungrateful that he was putting himself out for her?

He dug around until he found what he was looking for and returned to find her lying prone on the sand, her eyes closed. For a moment he registered her laboured breathing and the way it made her breasts rise and fall so rapidly. He noticed droplets of sea water drying into dots of salt on the faint curve of her belly and something shifted inside him. Something dark and powerful and strong. As he pulled out an old army knife and extracted a pair of tweezers, he realised his mouth had suddenly grown dry. 'You've got some spikes in your heel,' he said unevenly.

'You don't say?'

He gritted his teeth. What *was* her problem? 'Which I'm now going to remove.'

Her eyelids shot open as he spoke and as she stared at him he noticed her eyes for the first time. They were wary eyes, the colour of one of those wintry skies you sometimes saw over Paris. Beautiful eyes, he thought suddenly as another whisper of awareness rippled over his skin.

'Will it hurt?' she said.

'Probably. But there's no alternative. Are you brave?'

She shrugged. 'I suppose so.'

He almost smiled as he saw the defiant tilt of her chin. He wasn't used to prickly women. To women who were doing their damnedest *not* to react to him, even though the outline of her nipples against the stretched fabric of her bright bikini told a different story. 'What's your name?'

'Marnie. Marnie Porter.'

'Okay, Marnie Porter. Why don't you close your eyes again and try to relax while I remove the spikes?'

'*Relax?* Is that supposed to be a joke? Do you have any idea what this feels like?'

'Actually, I do. It happened to me some years ago. I'll be as gentle as I can.'

'I…*ouch*!' She glared at him, dark lashes fluttering like demented butterflies. 'If that's what you call being gentle, I'd hate to see you being rough!'

'Impossible to make it a completely pain-free experience, I'm afraid.'

'Oh, yeah?' She viewed him with a renewed look of suspicion. 'Are you a doctor, or something?'

Her random question was way off mark but

for some reason it pleased him. Mostly because it was rare to meet someone who didn't know who he was, who had no idea of all the baggage which came with having been born a Kanonidou. Even though he'd been away for a long time, the burden of his heritage never really left him and it came rushing back whenever he returned. And why *should* she know? She was obviously British—one of the thousands of tourists who visited this part of the world every year and spent the rest of their lives wistfully remembering its beauty. She wouldn't know about the intrigues of Greek society, or the fact that the lives of some of its better-known billionaires were not as unruffled as they appeared on the surface. 'No, I'm not a doctor. Do I look like one?'

'Not really,' she said, directing a pointed look at his faded jeans before closing her eyes again. 'More like a beach bum.'

As Leon's lips curved, he realised it was a long time since a woman had made him smile. He really *had* been working too hard. 'Am I hurting you?'

'A bit—but it's bearable.'

The biting of her lip indicated otherwise and Leon worked quickly to remove the last spike from her flesh, aware that she was clenching her fingers into white-knuckled fists.

'It's okay,' he said, at last. 'You can open your eyes now.'

Confronted again by that pewter gaze, he felt a wave of desire sweep over him as potent as anything he could ever remember. It made his heart pound. It made his groin ache with a rush of urgent need. It made him want to take her in his arms and kiss her. To lay her down in the sand and get physical with her.

As she sat up to examine her foot he was able to study her objectively, telling himself she was nothing special. Long, thick hair the colour of wet sand and killer curves contained in a very cheap bikini. But the shiny fabric looked good on her. Much better than it should have done. He was used to women who wore dazzling couture, not something which looked as if it had been picked up from a market stall. And wasn't it refreshing to see someone dressed in clothes which didn't cost the equivalent of a small national debt? A woman who didn't seem to care that her belly was a little rounded as she leaned over to survey his handiwork. A woman without diamonds, or gold, or bling.

'They've all gone!' she exclaimed.

'Yes,' he agreed gravely. 'They have.'

'Wow. Thank you.'

'It's nothing,' he said. 'But you should keep an eye on it. Make sure you keep it clean. Where are your shoes?'

'Over there.' She pointed to a small heap of clothing, sheltered by an overhanging rock.

'I'll get them for you.'

'There's no need.'

'I *said*, I'll get them for you.'

Marnie heard the ring of command in his voice, thinking, *This is someone who's used to being obeyed.* And although she didn't normally let herself get bossed around, there was no reason to object to what seemed like courtesy. Especially when he'd already gone out of his way to be so kind to her—and kindness could be compelling, she realised suddenly. Especially when you weren't used to it.

She watched as he headed towards her clothes, thinking that she could have watched him all day, because he was…magnificent. Tall and strong and rippling with muscle. Above the hard thrust of his thighs, his hips were narrow—the denim jeans clinging to the high curve of his buttocks, making her wonder what he might look like naked.

Her cheeks grew hot as she wondered

where on earth *that* had come from because she'd never even *seen* a naked man before! Not unless you counted those marble statues with tiny genitals in the museums which some of her more ambitious foster parents had dragged her round when she was younger, until they'd realised that she and her twin sister weren't ideal candidates for lessons in culture and had sent them packing back to the children's home.

The memory was more painful than it should have been and so Marnie forced her attention back to the man who had rescued her. His hair was damp and unruly black tendrils were dangling around his neck, making her itch to tame them into some kind of order. But she wanted other things, too. Things which had nothing to do with giving him an impromptu haircut. Things she'd never wanted before. Suddenly her breasts were aching and there was a strange, sweet clenching in her core.

She knew exactly what it was but the knowledge was freaking her out because she didn't *do* desire. Men left her cold—they always had—even gorgeous men like this one. She was employed by an upmarket unisex hair salon in London and met plenty of lookers in the course of her working week, but to Marnie they were just pretty wallpaper. She didn't trust beauty. Actually, she didn't place her trust in much at all because too many times she'd had it thrown back in her face.

He bent to retrieve her clothing and she wished she hadn't been so caught up in her daydreams. Because when he turned he caught her staring and as their eyes met something passed between them—a wordless sensation which slid over her skin like honey. And it was weird. On some fundamental level it was almost as if she recognised him. As if he were capable of knowing her like no other man ever could, even though they'd never met before. She shook her head. She was going mad. She must be. Now might be the moment to stop reading those time-slip novels she loved so much. Either that or the strain of the past few months had finally caught up with her.

And it still isn't over, she reminded herself bitterly. *In fact, it has barely begun.*

She started to scramble to her feet but he must have seen her sway because as he reached her, he extended his hand to support her.

'Hey,' he said softly. 'Watch out.'

Those fingers which had ministered so expertly to her foot were now cupping her elbow and although Marnie wanted to revel in the sweet sensation of having him touch her, she forced herself to draw away.

'I'm fine,' she said stiffly, waving away his attempts to help as she wriggled into her loose-fitting T-shirt dress. Gingerly, she slid her injured foot into one sandal, then put on the other and gave her head a quick shake, feeling the warmth of her drying hair as it brushed against her back. 'Right. Well, that's all done. I ought to get going. Thanks again for coming to my aid. I'm very…grateful.'

Leon told himself to let her go. She had managed to find her way down to this small private beach on her own, so presumably she could make her own way back again. He glanced at the discreet golden and coral sign of the upmarket Paradeisos hotel complex which hung in front of a coded wooden gate, and idly wondered if she was trespassing. Probably.

Should he offer her a lift to where she was staying? His final duty done and his conscience fully satisfied as he saw her safely home?

But her hair was almost dry now and he re-

alised it wasn't the colour of wet sand at all.
It was as pale as silver. As moonlight.

His voice wasn't quite steady as he spoke.
It was as uneven as that of a teenage boy who
had just realised how a woman could make
him feel. Blood was pounding powerfully at
all his pulse points and a sense of being properly *alive* flooded through him. 'I could give
you a lift back if you like,' he said. 'Better
still, I could drive you round the island first.
Have you seen much of it?'

She shrugged, before lifting her gaze to his.
'Not as much as I'd like. The trouble is that I
work long hours and I often work on my day
off because…'

'Because?'

She shook her head. 'It doesn't matter. I
went on a round-the-island coach trip when
I first arrived but we didn't see very much
of it. The organiser seemed more concerned
with getting us to buy vases than wanting to
show us the place.'

He shuddered. 'I know those vases.'

'Ugly.'

'*Neh*. As you say, ugly. Yet this island has
her secrets. Places where the tourists tend not
to go. We could drive through some of the
villages. Watch the sunset from the Dhas-

sos Rock. Maybe find ourselves something to eat.'

Her grey eyes regarded him suspiciously and this was definitely *not* a reaction he was used to.

'Are you asking me to have dinner with you?'

'Sure. Why not?'

'Well, for a start, I don't even know your name.'

Conditioned by a lifetime of expectations, Leon felt an instinctive tension enter his body. 'It's Leonidas. Leonidas Kanonidou.' He watched for some sort of reaction but when there was none, he relaxed a little. 'Most people call me Leon.'

'Like a lion,' she said slowly.

'Exactly like a lion. Do you speak Greek?'

'Very funny. That would be the hardest thing in the world.'

No, not quite the hardest, he thought ruefully, aware of the exquisite throb at his groin. 'So, now you know who I am, are you going to have dinner with me?'

She didn't answer straight away and even her hesitation was a turn-on. He was used to capitulation. To women being available at the metaphorical snap of his fingers. To being hit on—sometimes subtly, sometimes not. His growing reputation as one of the world's most eligible men had contributed to his recent absence from the dating scene, his appetite jaded by too much choice and too much opportunity.

What Leon wasn't used to was being kept waiting, because people went out of their way to please him. As if his gratitude would somehow improve the quality of their lives. Hoping he would give them a break, or a job, or a wedding ring. He was used to people laughing at his jokes, even if they weren't funny—which wasn't often. Was this what happened to men who were not billionaires, he wondered idly—were they judged on their merits rather than the size of their wallet? Was this unknown Englishwoman destined to be remembered as the only woman who had ever turned him down?

But she didn't.

Of course she didn't.

'Okay.' She shrugged. 'Why not?'

Her reluctance was possibly contrived—yet Leon didn't care. He seemed to have stopped caring about anything right now, other than this diminutive woman with attitude. He watched her lift her arms to tie her hair back then almost wished she hadn't because it drew his attention to the heavy curve of her breasts. Had she been intending to showcase the nipples which had tightened so enticingly and was she aware of her power over him at that moment? Another surge of hunger flooded through him, which was crazy.

Crazy.

He thought about the busy timetable for the weekend ahead. The selected cream of young Grecian society would be in attendance, eager to participate in the lavish events lined up for them. There certainly hadn't been many slots available to accommodate the reckless acquisition of a new lover he'd only just met. Plus, there would be an available slew of far more suitable hook-ups than this spiky blonde with the wintry eyes. Leon swallowed. Maybe this wasn't such a good idea after all.

But common sense was no match for the heavy slug of his heart or the growing heat of his blood. It certainly wasn't powerful enough to stop him grabbing his T-shirt from the back of his motorbike and pulling it roughly over a body which once again was exquisitely aroused.

'Then let's go,' he said roughly.

CHAPTER TWO

'So what do you think? Like it?'

The drawled questions, delivered in Leon Kanonidou's knockout velvety voice made Marnie's cheeks grow hot and, hoping he hadn't noticed—she looked around the restaurant.

It was gorgeous. Like something you might see in a film. Just a few tables perched on a dramatic rocky outcrop above the sea, into which the sun was sinking like a giant red ball. Beneath them was a long beach of fine sand, lit crimson and mauve by the dying light. Still early, the place was empty except for them—though surprisingly for such an out-of-the-way location, every table was reserved. In fact, the proprietor had borne down on them rather forbiddingly when they'd arrived, all windswept and dishevelled and she'd thought they were going to be turned away. Until Leon had spoken to him in Greek and Marnie had watched an astonishing transformation take place. The man had almost done a double take before nodding his head, quickly removing a 'Reserved' notice and reverentially ushering them to the table with the best view.

Marnie thought she could understand why. Had her companion used his lazy charm to get what he wanted, or had he simply turned on the full force of his charismatic personality which made it hard to imagine refusing him anything?

She felt supremely relaxed, sitting here with him. The tiny place had none of the unashamed opulence of the Paradeisos complex where she worked, which sometimes made her feel a little bit uncomfortable. Yet as she shifted her bottom on the chair, she found herself wondering what she *was* comfortable with—because climbing onto the back of a total stranger's motorbike and speeding off in a cloud of dust wasn't her kind of thing at all.

Usually she was cautious with men and as unlike her twin sister as it was possible to be. She had never acted impetuously with a member of the opposite sex because up until now there hadn't been a good reason. Was feeling as if someone had reached inside her body to stir up her senses a good enough reason? As Leon's eyes met hers she saw his lips curve into a faintly mocking smile—almost as if he'd guessed at her thoughts. Yet instead of bristling defensively, Marnie found herself grinning back and that was addictive too. For a moment she felt as if she were somebody else. One of her clients, maybe. One of those rich, confident women who breezed into the salon and seemed to smile for no reason at all. Who studied their phones with expressions of pleasure, not dread. She stared down at the dish of shiny olives and wondered if it would be wise to eat one before deciding to err on the side of caution because black teeth were never a good look, except maybe at Halloween.

Instead she sat back and luxuriated in the fact that for the first time since she'd been on Paramenios, she actually felt as if she were on holiday.

Leon had driven her all the way round the tiny island, past postcard images of sleepy white villages with purple bougainvillea scrambling around bright blue doors. She'd marvelled at crystalline turquoise waters fringed with unexpected greenery and the soar of distant mountains. They'd skirted tiny shops bursting with trays of ripe, plump peaches, and seen lines of drying octopi, which stretched in front of the dancing sea. Yet all the time she had been acutely aware of the Greek's hard body as she clung to his waist. Had found herself *grateful* that her pillion position gave her a legitimate excuse to wrap her arms around him and feel all that hard muscle rippling beneath his black T-shirt. Which came as a bit of a shock to someone who wasn't remotely tactile. Who found it hard not to recoil if someone touched her. The truth was that she'd never met a man she considered irresistible.

But Leon Kanonidou was another matter...

And now, sitting opposite him sipping a delicious drink he'd told her was made from almonds and cinnamon, she luxuriated in the sensation of being happy in her own skin. Until she remembered Pansy, miserable and scared in her prison cell in England, and a shiver of guilt ran down her spine.

Aware that Leon was regarding her expectantly as if awaiting a reply to his question, she dragged her thoughts back to the present. 'I love it,' she said. 'It's the prettiest restaurant I've ever seen.'

'And does it make up for the coach trip to see the vases?'

'Oh, I think you could definitely say that. Not an ugly vase in sight.'

He smiled, lifting his fingertips to summon a waiter, but the proprietor himself came scurrying over, nodding his head intently while the order was given in Greek.

Once the man had departed, Leon leaned back in his chair. 'I've ordered fish. I hope you like it. It's the only thing on the menu.'

She hesitated, aware that so far he had made all the decisions and although she was quite enjoying somebody else being in charge for a change, maybe it was time she asserted herself. She looked at him with challenge in her eyes. 'What would you say if I said I hated it?'

'I'd say you'd never eaten fresh fish which had been hauled out of the water just a few hours before and then thrown on a fire scented with herbs fresh from the mountain-side, so that the flesh is as soft as butter melting in your mouth.'

His voice was caressing now and Marnie was suddenly aware of the weight of her hair as it fell over her breasts and the sweet, tight tug of her nipples. And suddenly Pansy was forgotten. Everything was forgotten except for the way he was looking at her and making her feel. Was that why she blurted out her next words, which afterwards would make her cringe for being so unbelievably naïve? 'You make everything sound so...'

'So?'

His gaze pierced through her like a blue sword aimed straight at her heart. Marnie wanted to say *romantic*, but suspected that wasn't the right word. Because romance was soft, wasn't it? And there was nothing soft about this man, no matter how silken his question. There was something hard and invulnerable about him—something which attracted yet cautioned her at the same time. She wanted him to kiss her, she realised. She wanted it in a way which was inexplicable— yet she didn't know a thing about him. She smiled up at the proprietor as a delicious-looking platter of sizzling fish was deposited on the table, alongside a bowl of Greek salad and two plates.

'Why don't you tell me something about yourself?' she said, her years as a hairdresser reminding her that people liked nothing better than to talk about themselves.

'*Ohi.*' He shook his head, tendrils of dark

hair moving sinuously against the olive glow of his skin. 'I'm far more interested in you, Marnie Porter. Who you are and how you came to be here.'

She felt a sudden rush of nerves, though she kept her face impassive—the result of years of knowing that social workers would be studying your expression and trying to work out what you were really thinking. But Marnie didn't want to talk about her past, which had been rubbish. She didn't want to consider the equally scary future either, with all the worrying possibilities which lay ahead. She just wanted this. Now. Whatever *this* was. So she stalled. She was an old hand at stalling. 'What exactly do you want to know?'

'You're English?'

'Yes, I am. From London. Well, Acton.'

'Act On,' he repeated, making it sound like two words instead of one. 'I know London very well but I don't think I've heard of Act On.'

'There's no reason why you should—it's hardly in the buzzing epicentre of the city, though there is a transport museum, which is very popular with schoolboys.'

'But not with you, I think?'

'No. Not with me.'

He smiled as a waiter slid a sizzling fish onto each of their plates, before raising his dark eyebrows at her. 'And this is your first time in Greece?'

She nodded. 'It is.'

'Where are you staying?'

'You don't think I could be staying where you found me?' she questioned innocently. 'At the Paradeisos? Don't I look like their usual type of client?'

There was a pause. 'If you want the truth, then no.'

Marnie stiffened because this was familiar territory. Who could blame her for being defensive when she'd been considered second-best for most of her life? Being second-best was the reason she'd worn hand-me-down clothes and shoes. And why she'd been stuck in the homes of people who didn't really want her, or her sister. 'Too trashy, I suppose?' she demanded hotly.

But he shook his tousled head. 'No, not at all. Too…normal, I guess.'

Oh, how wrong could he be? *Normal?* Marnie almost laughed. An outsider, yes. And a freak too, very occasionally. Both those things. But a human being who blended in with the rest of the world? Never.

'I *am* staying there, if you must know,' she countered, enjoying the surprise which flickered over his face. And then, because he had been kind to her and because she liked him, she shrugged before making her admission. 'I work there. In the spa.'

'You work there?'

'That's right. I'm a hairdresser, though I'm also qualified as a manicurist and a beauty therapist. And obviously I can do brows and waxing. Not my favourite part of the job, I have to admit.' She pulled a face. 'Whoops. Probably too much information.'

Leon felt a rush of something he didn't recognise. Was it her deadpan delivery which was making him smile, or her refreshing outspokenness? She certainly wasn't the usual kind of woman he had dinner with. He mixed with investment bankers and CEOs. With models who commanded a king's ransom for photographers to capture their matchless faces and incredible bodies. With actresses who kept gold-plated awards rather pretentiously on the shelves of their downstairs closet.

And usually he would be bored out of his skull by this stage of the meal.

He felt his pulse quicken as he acknowledged the steely throb at his groin. She wasn't his usual *type*, that was for sure—and not just because she was blonde. She was pretty enough. Not beautiful, no—the set of her jaw was too firm and her lips weren't full enough for conventional beauty—though her dark-lashed eyes were remarkable. She was no traf-fic-stopper, yet there was something about her which was so out of his comfort zone that Leon felt curiously *alive* in her company.

'A hairdresser,' he observed softly.

She pursed her lips together, as if he had criticised her. 'I'm actually a very good hair-dresser, which is how I got a job in a place like the Paradeisos, which—in case you didn't know—is a very high-end hotel complex.'

'Yes, it is,' he agreed gravely.

'In fact, I can give you a trim some time, if you like. Those ends don't look in great con-dition to me and it's long enough for you to be able to lose a bit. Call it payback for hav-ing come to my aid, if you like.'

Leon nearly laughed as he wondered how the prohibitively expensive hairdressers he visited in London and Paris and New York would react to the suggestion that his hair wasn't being properly maintained. 'Maybe I'll take you up on that,' he murmured. 'But in the meantime—don't you think we should eat? Any minute now and the chef will come storming over here to demand to know what's wrong with the food.'

She looked startled. As if she had forgotten that they were in a restaurant and that the proprietor was casting worried looks over their untouched meal.

'I guess we should,' she said.

But he noticed that she was spooning salad onto her plate without enthusiasm, and chewing fish in a way which seemed almost mechanical. Did the food taste like sawdust on her tongue, as it did for him? Yet that should come as no surprise when eating was the last thing he needed right now. He wondered if she was aware that he wanted to taste nothing more complex than her skin. To slowly lick his tongue over every salt-covered atom of her curvy body, to discover her scent and her flavour.

Yet he didn't *do* casual hook-ups. It didn't suit his fastidious nature. Maybe it was arrogant of him to think that his cool intellect was always capable of conquering his baser instincts, because hadn't he been on fire with need since she'd slid onto the back of his bike? Hadn't it taken all the concentration he possessed—which was usually formidable—to focus on the journey and not the heavy throb between his legs? As an exercise in self-control, it had been considerable.

'Your turn now,' she said.

Her words shattered his erotic fantasy. 'My turn?' he questioned throatily.

'I don't really know anything about you, do I? Other than the fact you were named after a lion and you're very handy with a pair of tweezers.'

He started to laugh. Maybe *that* was the secret of her unexpected allure. She was quick-tongued. Bright. Plus she was treating him with an irreverence he wasn't used to, which he was discovering he liked. Would she continue to behave in the same way towards him once she discovered who he really was? He doubted it.

All the more reason not to tell her.

'I'm Greek,' he informed her.

'Obviously.'

'And I came to Paramenios for the weekend because work has been pretty full-on lately.'

He watched as she bit into a slice of tomato and found himself wanting to lick away the gleam of juice which lingered on her lips.

'What kind of work do you do?'

The question was unwelcome and Leon wondered how to avoid it. If he told her, it would change everything. It always did. His billionaire status altered the way women viewed him—hadn't that been demonstrated time after time, and contributed to his innate cynicism?

'I'm a builder,' he said.

'Ah. I *thought* so!'

'You did?'

'Uh-huh.' Pushing away her barely touched plate, she smiled. 'I can imagine you wielding a sledgehammer on a building site. You've definitely got the build for it—no joke intended.'

For some reason, Leon found her remark slightly insulting. Was she implying he was all brawn and no brains? For a moment he was tempted to tell her that he'd been offered a place at Stanford at a precociously young age, until he'd decided that his future didn't lie in academia and he needed to get out there and make some money. But then he wondered what he was thinking. This wasn't some sort of boasting exercise. He certainly wasn't there in order to establish his intellectual credentials, or *prove* himself to her. He knew exactly why he was there—and judging from the sexual energy which had been fizzing between them from the get-go, she knew it too.

'Have you finished?' he asked.

She surveyed her plate. 'Well, I have and I haven't. I really don't want to offend the chef, but I'm not hungry.'

'Me, neither.'

'Must be the heat.'

'Must be.' There was a long pause. 'Don't worry about the chef,' he said softly. 'We'll make sure we tip generously.'

'Yes. Yes, of course.' Hastily, she reached for her beach bag and a sandy shell fell onto the table as she started to rummage around inside. 'I'll get my purse—when I can find it, that is. I'm happy to split the bill.'

Leon's eyes narrowed. It was a novel experience to have a woman offer to pay and for a moment he thought about letting her, because novel experiences were rare in his world. Until he reminded himself that despite the clifftop restaurant's deceptively rustic appearance, the food commanded prices far beyond the reach of most mortals. He shook his head. 'No, you won't—but thanks for the offer. I'll see to it.'

'But—'

'I *said*, I'll pay. Now, would you like to look at the desserts before I ask for the check, or would you prefer to walk on the beach and catch the last of the sunset?'

His words floated on the warm air and as Marnie stared into his sculpted face, she was unbearably tempted. Until he'd suggested it, she hadn't been aware of just how much she wanted to be alone with him—away from the frankly intrusive glances of the attendant staff who seemed to be hovering around their table quite unnecessarily in her opinion, considering they were the only customers in the place.

But she wasn't stupid and she knew how the world worked. If it were possible for a person to be aware of the corrupting power of sex without ever having had any actual experience of it—then Marnie *was* that person. She had been brought up to fear it. To be aware of all the trouble it could get a woman into. It was why it hadn't particularly bothered her when men had accused her of being frigid or cold, whenever she'd failed to respond to their fumbling kisses. But those kisses had felt like ambushes, whereas the thought of Leon's lips pressing down on hers was making her feel quite dizzy with need.

He was making it clear that he found her attractive and maybe she should be scared by the knowledge of where that could lead. Maybe she should tell him that if he wanted to see her again, then he should take her number and call her and then arrange a second date. That was what you were *supposed* to do, wasn't it?

But she wasn't going to.

Because Marnie knew better than anyone how fleeting happiness could be and something was telling her that if she didn't grab at whatever he was offering, she might never get the chance again. Why *wouldn't* she want to take a walk with this gorgeous man whose black waves tumbled so riotously against his darkly golden skin?

Which was why she nodded. Why she rose to her feet with a solemn expression. Why she accepted that she was about to break one of her most fundamental rules—and break it big time. 'I'd like that very much.' Her fingers tightened around the strap of her beach bag. 'I'll just use the bathroom and then I'm all yours.'

Her words were clumsy and open to mis-interpretation and she wished she could take them back. But there again, why should she?

They both knew what was on the menu for tonight and it certainly wasn't fish and salad.

CHAPTER THREE

HIS LIPS WERE SOFT. Surprisingly soft. Marnie had thought they would be hard. Hard like his body. Hard like the fierce blue glint of his eyes. But what did she know, other than when Leon Kanonidou pulled her into his arms it felt as if this were the reason she'd been born?

They had left the restaurant and walked slowly along the sand, the pain in her heel gradually receding as they watched the setting sun make its slow descent in the sky before finally slipping into the sea. Their arms brushing occasionally, they had commented on the soft sound of the waves and the fiery glow of the dying embers. But that conversation had felt *mechanical*, rather than natural, and it had filled Marnie with all kinds of fears—the main one being that she had totally misjudged the situation and maybe the attraction she felt for him was one-sided.

She'd found herself wishing he would touch her. But he hadn't. They'd just walked and walked until all the daylight had disappeared and faint stars had begun to puncture the moonless sky, before turning to retrace their steps towards his motorbike. And the more he had kept his distance, the more she had wanted him.

They had turned to retrace their steps and Marnie had seen the restaurant in the distance—all brightly lit up like a cruise liner. They must have started playing music after they'd left but as they stopped to listen to the faint chords of a bouzouki drifting on the warm air, she had been acutely aware of a sinking sense of disappointment.

So was this *it*? Was her determination to do something wild and free for the first time in her life about to amount to nothing, because the man she was with wasn't interested in her? Maybe he really had just been acting as an impromptu guide, eager to show the English tourist the hidden delights of Paramenios.

And then, almost as if he'd read her mind, Leon caught hold of her and turned her round, his hands on either side of her waist. She held her breath because his touch felt *electric* and he studied her upturned face for what felt like a long time, before lowering his head to kiss her.

It was...dynamite.

It was...life-changing.

Marnie swayed in disbelief, her limbs growing instantly boneless. How was it possible for a kiss to feel this *good*? How could *anything* feel this good? At first there was barely any contact between them—just the intoxicating graze of his mouth over hers. Did he know how desperately frustrating that was? Was that why he deepened the kiss so that, suddenly, everything changed? The pressure of his lips became seeking. Supercharged and somehow *profound*. As if she were the sleeping princess in the pages of a fairy story, who had been woken by a gorgeous prince.

He deepened the kiss and began to stroke one of her breasts. Her nipple was pushing against her baggy T-shirt dress towards the circling of his thumb. She could feel the syrupy rush to her bikini bottoms and realised she wanted him to touch her there, too. She wanted things she'd never wanted before and she wanted them very badly. Was it that which made her writhe her hips against his with instinctive hunger, causing him to utter something in Greek which sounded almost *despairing*?

The sound broke the spell and she drew back, though in the faint light all she could see was the hectic glitter of his eyes. 'What... what did you just say?'

'I said that you set my blood on fire, *agape mou*. And that I want you very much. But you already know that.'

Well, she knew he wanted her, yes. She wasn't actually sure about the 'blood on fire' bit, because nobody had ever said anything like that to her before. And although she liked it, her instinct was not to believe him because even if they were true, she knew compliments always came with a price.

Yet what was the *point* of all this if she was just going to pepper the experience with her usual doubts, and spoil it? Couldn't she have a holiday from her normal self and shake off all the worries which had been weighing her down for so long? Couldn't she be a different Marnie tonight—one who was seeking nothing but uncomplicated pleasure? She had always been the responsible one. The one who looked out for other people, always preparing herself for the shadows which inevitably hovered just out of sight. Wasn't it time to articulate what *she* wanted for a change?

She cleared her throat. 'Would you mind speaking in English so I can understand what you're saying?'

She could hear the amusement which deepened his voice.

'Are we planning to do a lot of talking then, Marnie? Is that what turns you on?'

Something warned her she'd be straying into dangerous territory if she told him she didn't *know* what turned her on because she'd never given herself the chance to find out. But while she didn't want to lie to him, that didn't mean she couldn't tell a different kind of truth.

'*You* turn me on,' she said boldly and something about the breathless rush of her words made his powerful body tense.

'Oh, *do* I?' he questioned, tilting her chin with his fingers so that their darkened gazes clashed. 'So what are we going to do about that, I wonder?'

She didn't dare answer in case she said the wrong thing. In case she frightened him away with her appalling lack of experience—because her gorgeous biker looked and kissed like someone who knew his way around the block. So instead, she just did what she'd been aching to do all evening, which was to touch his face—grazing her fingertips down over its sculpted planes, as if she were committing them to memory.

Did his quick intake of breath mean he liked it—was that why he pulled her back into his arms and hauled her up close to his body, so that they felt glued together? Her nipples were stony and she could feel the hot slick of desire between her legs. As he moulded the curve of her buttocks with his open palms, she became aware of the rocky outline of his erection, which was pressing through the soft denim of his jeans against her.

'Can you feel how much I want you?' he taunted softly.

Maybe she should have been daunted by all that virile power, but weirdly enough she wasn't. Because it all seemed so *natural*. As if it was meant to be. As if her life up until now had been nothing but a preparation for this moment. 'Yes,' she breathed. 'Yes, I can.'

His fingertips were hovering close to the hemline of her dress. 'I want to see you,' he husked. 'I want to see your body, Marnie.'

Marnie closed her eyes. She could hear the raw hunger underpinning his words and sense the barely restrained need in them. And didn't that match her own hunger and make it easy to know how to respond to him, despite her pitiful innocence? No need to point out that the moonless night would make twenty-twenty vision impossible and it would be practically impossible for him to see her with any degree of detail. 'I'm not stopping you,' she whispered boldly. 'Go ahead.'

'*Meta haras.*' His words sounded like dark honey coating her skin with sweetness. With a fluid movement he peeled the dress over her head and let it fall to the sand, one-handedly unclipping the fastening of her now-dry bikini top, so that her breasts came tumbling free. And if at times Marnie had despaired about her disproportionately large bust, Leon Kanonidou's murmur of appreciation was enough to banish those complaints for ever.

'My turn, I think,' he said, pulling off his T-shirt and dropping it to the ground, so that his torso was as bare as hers.

He pulled her into his arms and that first contact of skin against skin felt so delicious that Marnie gave a little gurgle of joy. He was smoothing his fingers through her hair. He was kissing her and kissing her, until once again she was in that blissful state of molten compliance. He slid his fingers between her legs and she held her breath as they pushed aside the panel of her bikini bottoms—terrified he was going to stop his intimate exploration.

But he didn't stop.

He started to stroke his fingers over her and a ragged moan escaped from her lips.

Maybe it was the shock of discovery which made her so instantly responsive or maybe it was the things he was saying to her, some in English and some in Greek. She no longer cared which language he was using—all she cared about was the way he was making her feel. That sweet, savage tightening in her groin and exquisite aching of her breasts. Her heart was racing as waves of something unbearably beautiful beckoned her towards an unknown destination. The tension grew and her body felt so taut that she didn't think she could bear it any longer. And then she went under—or was it over?

His kiss drowned out her spiralling cries of pleasure as Marnie began to spasm around his finger, trying like mad to hold onto the feeling until her body gradually grew still. She was dimly aware of him supporting her weight while he bent to smooth his T-shirt over the sand to form a makeshift sheet—admittedly on the small side—before very gently easing her down on top of it. His shadow fell over her as his hand went to the button of his jeans and the image was reminiscent of when she'd seen him on the beach earlier. And that was when reality hit her befuddled brain with a bombardment of urgent questions.

You realise what you're about to do? You're about to have sex with a man you barely know. All those things which have scared you all your life are right here. Things you were determined never to do. Things you know you shouldn't do.

That reality hit should have been enough to make her stop but it wasn't. Because as he slithered out of his jeans, Marnie was able to ignore the voice of her conscience by noticing several things. Firstly, that he wasn't wearing any underpants—which seemed more erotic than shocking. Secondly, that he was withdrawing a foil packet from his back pocket— making her wonder if he *always* carried a condom with him. And if that were the case— then didn't that make her just one in a long line of conquests of women he barely knew?

But those discoveries were quickly eclipsed

by another—which was that she had been completely wrong about the available light. Because while there was no moon, the sky of Paramenios was incredibly clear and the millions of stars were certainly bright enough to illuminate Leon Kanonidou's magnificent body. Twenty-twenty vision it might not be, but the starlight was strong enough to emphasise the rippling muscles and honed flesh. She gazed at the hair-roughened chest and narrow hips, which led down to those long, powerful legs coated in a silvery gleam.

Naked, Leon Kanonidou was the most beautiful sight she'd ever seen. Even the proud pale pole of his erection springing from a dark blur of hair wasn't enough to daunt the innocent Marnie as she opened her arms to him.

Her soft curves accommodated his hard planes and sculpted limbs as if they'd been designed for that purpose. Was it always like this? she wondered dizzily as he moved over her. So...*easy*? His lips began to explore her skin, his tongue sliding over her as if he had all the time in the world ahead of him. He licked her nipples and belly and then the delicate skin between her thighs and she shivered. His fingers moved to reacquaint themselves with the slickness between her legs, feathering her with that dextrous touch which made her feel as if she were drowning in sweetness. Should she be doing something back? she wondered. Actively participate by touching *him*, even though her clumsy movements might give away the fact that he was with a novice?

But while she was plucking up the courage to curl her fingers around his rocky shaft, he dissolved all rational thought by kissing her again.

'You taste salty,' he murmured, against her lips.

'So do you,' she murmured back—and something about that small interchange felt as intimate as anything else they'd done and filled her with a newfound confidence, so that when he reached for the condom which lay on the sand beside them, Marnie felt nothing but eager for what was about to happen. She watched as he stroked on the protection, his starlit expression a study in concentration until he had sheathed himself, his lazy smile of complicity emphasising the closeness of the moment.

'Now, where was I?'

He was right here. Holding her, and stroking her, and Marnie was touching him back and he was almost purring with pleasure. His fingers were tangled in her hair and his body was pressing down on hers so that she could feel the soft sand at her back. There was a sudden rapid escalation of need and a subtle shift in tension and her thighs parted eagerly as if some unseen force was choreographing her movements. She held her breath as he made that first deep thrust inside her, her quick cry the only indication that pain had momentarily eclipsed the pleasure.

But Leon must have heard it. Or felt it. Or something. Because he stilled inside her, and when she looked up into his face all she could see was confusion glinting from his narrowed eyes.

'Please don't stop,' she whispered, and afterwards she would be ashamed at having said that. For *pleading* with him, almost.

But his answer took her by surprise.

'I can't stop,' he said, almost bitterly, and began to move again.

She'd thought that this unmistakable disconnect would be enough to shatter the magic so that she would feel nothing—but she had been wrong. Because Leon immediately adapted to what he'd just discovered by moving inside her at a completely changed pace. At first, his thrusts were performed with almost exaggerated care, until her newly awakened body had adjusted itself to the rocky width of him and to what was happening to her. He took it slow. So very slow. Until she had completely relaxed.

'Oh, Leon,' she cried out.

Until that sweet urgency had flared up inside her again, building into such a pitch until she could hold it back no longer. And this time when she came, his body bucked in perfect time with hers.

But this time he did not kiss her quiet.

Leon rolled off Marnie's soft body with a reluctance which unsettled him even more than what he had just discovered. He wanted to feel anger and indignation. He wanted to accuse her of misrepresentation. Yet all he could think about was the moment when he'd entered her—recalling that fleeting sensation of resistance before being encased in her molten tightness. He had wanted a novel experience, he reminded himself bitterly. Well, this one had certainly ticked all the right boxes. Or the wrong ones. He gazed up into the star-punctured vault of the black sky and even though he told himself he wasn't in the least bit interested in her motivations, he found himself biting out a single word.

'Why?'

'Why what?' she questioned, her voice soft and replete.

He rolled onto his side to look at her and instantly regretted the action, for her cushioned flesh looked utterly inviting and he could detect the musky perfume of her sex on the air. Leon swallowed, hovering on the brink of unbearable temptation. He wanted to touch those peaking breasts again. He wanted to part those silken folds and plunge into her with the erection which was already growing rigid against his belly.

'You were a virgin!' he accused.

Her eyes fluttered open. 'So what?'

'Are you kidding me? Virgins don't just have random sex on beaches with men they've just met.'

'You mean, they should save it for their wedding night?' Her laugh was tinged with a cynicism he recognised as something regularly found in his own repertoire. She sat up, her hair falling over her breasts. 'Oh, don't worry, Leon—you can wipe that look of horror from your face. I'm not about to start demanding you provide me with a gold ring and white dress!'

'Because I'd say the white dress would be redundant by now, wouldn't you?' he drawled.

'And a marriage would be a lot harder to walk away from than this!'

He watched as she scrambled to her feet with an innate sexiness which made him want to pull her back down again, but she cursed as she put her weight onto her injured foot and, instinctively, he frowned. 'Careful with that foot.'

'Just leave my damned foot out of it, will you?'

He wished he could. He wished he'd never heard her stricken scream. He wished he were a million miles away from here, but he felt a responsibility towards her—one he didn't want, but which he would honour. It was the least he could do in the circumstances. Rising to his feet, he reached for his jeans. 'You'd better get dressed,' he said abruptly. 'I'll take you back.'

'That won't be necessary!' Speaking through gritted teeth, she stepped into her bikini bottoms and hauled them up over her hips. 'I certainly don't need your grudging charity. Don't worry about it. I can make my own way back.'

The sting of pride in her words made him feel an unexpected wash of gentleness towards her. 'Marnie,' he said patiently. 'It's getting late and you're in one of the most remote parts of the island. How are you proposing to get back on your own? It's not like we're in Act On. There isn't a reliable bus service.'

'You've obviously never been to Acton, or you'd know that reliable is the last word you could ever use to describe our bus service!'

He could see her struggling to do up her bikini top and instinctively reached out to help her but she batted him away. 'I can do it myself. Though I expect you're far more practised at it than I am!'

Half in amusement, he watched while she fumbled with the clip until her magnificent breasts were constrained once more, and then pulled on the rather ugly T-shirt dress, which successfully concealed all her curvy magnificence. Lastly, she shook her hair and ran her fingers through it, but still it looked wild and indescribably sexy as she turned to face him. She was struggling to control her rapid breathing and appeared to be choosing her words with care. 'Look, what just happened was obviously a huge mistake.'

'It's done now,' he returned, slightly irritated by the less than flattering sentiment. Was she trying to imply that she hadn't enjoyed it? Or that she regretted it? 'You're sure you're okay?'

'Well, it doesn't hurt, if that's what you mean,' she responded bluntly. 'Or is this the moment when I'm supposed to pour on copious amounts of praise about your skill as a lover?'

Easing the zip over his hardness with difficulty, he winced. 'That is what usually happens.'

'Oh!'

For a moment he thought she was going to launch herself at him and start drumming her fists against his chest and wasn't there a part of him which wanted her to do that, because the fury on her face was turning him on more than it should have done and if she attacked him then surely he would be justified in kissing her? Yet even as he rejected such a scenario as folly, Leon couldn't shake off the sensation of being…cheated. Feeling as if she had lured him into a honey trap with the skills of an ancient siren. Lured him into something he'd been having second thoughts about and then delivered something he hadn't been expecting.

All through dinner he had acknowledged the powerful chemistry sizzling between them, but during their walk on the beach he had forced good sense to prevail. As the soft sand had ridged between his bare toes, he had silently listed the reasons why making love to Marnie Porter was a bad idea—and there were plenty. They were strangers. They were from different worlds. It was why he hadn't kissed her. Why he had walked chastely by her side even though he had been aching with desire and frustration, and her body language had indicated she felt the same way.

Yet as the throbbing in his groin had become unbearable, he had wondered just who he was protecting. Just because he'd never done a casual hookup before, didn't mean it couldn't happen. He wanted it and she wanted it. Where was the problem? They were both adults. But he'd *assumed* she was similarly experienced. Why wouldn't he? He had always steered clear of virgins—and for precisely the reasons she had sarcastically joked about. Because women didn't just give their innocence to a passing stranger, did they—

not without wanting something in return? Especially when the stranger in question possessed riches beyond most people's wildest dreams.

His mouth flattened. Maybe *he* was the one who was being naïve, not her. Maybe she *did* know his true identity and she had been saving herself for someone from whom she could reap some very attractive benefits. Someone with money. He shook his head. Wouldn't it be almost easier if that *were* the case? If he were able to place her into the well-worn compartment in his life labelled *gold-digger*? But deep down he didn't really believe that. There was something too proud about her to let him believe she was motivated by greed.

Yet whatever her intentions had been, it mustn't happen again. Because for all her bravado, Leon had detected an unmistakable trace of tenderness when she had opened her arms to him. And because he hadn't been expecting that either, it had thrown him. He had briefly lost himself in her softness, disorientated by a swirl of conflicting and unrecognisable emotions, which had troubled him. He was the only man she'd ever had sex with, he reminded himself, and, despite her insolence towards him afterwards, she would inevitably read too much into it. Women always did. They were experts at seeing what they wanted to see. At obscuring and manipulating the truth if it didn't fit in with their own needs.

His jaw tightened. Hadn't he learnt that to his own detriment—and hadn't the fallout turned him into a man who had been accused too often of having a lump of ice for a heart? He was certainly not the kind of person this little innocent should be associating with.

So he would make her realise she would be better off without him. And the sooner she was out of his life, the sooner he would forget her.

Digging into the back pocket of his jeans for his keys, he turned to her—steeling himself against the soft quivering bow of her lips, made silver by the starlight. 'Grab your helmet, Marnie,' he instructed coldly. 'I'll take you back to the hotel.'

CHAPTER FOUR

'MARNIE, YOU'RE GOING to have to do an emergency manicure!'

Marnie glanced up, emerging from the uncomfortable swirl of her thoughts to focus on her boss, a wiry and very dynamic Scotswoman called Jodie, who had worked on Paramenios for almost a decade. It was Jodie who'd been responsible for getting her this prestigious summer job on a Greek island and Jodie who had persuaded her salon in London to allow her to have unpaid leave for the summer so she could double or even triple her salary in this luxury resort. Thus it was important not to annoy someone who'd done her a number of favours. But, really, how on earth could a manicure ever be described as an emergency?

'Can't someone else do it?' Marnie questioned. 'I'm not feeling that great, to be honest.'

'Yeah, I can tell. You look terrible,' said Jodie bluntly. 'What happened?'

Marnie bit her lip, because how could she possibly confide the reason for her washed-out appearance or inability to concentrate for most of the morning? She could just imagine Jodie's reaction if she explained that yesterday she'd met a gorgeous stranger, had let him take her to dinner—then ended up losing her virginity to him on a beach. Or that he'd dropped her off near her staff accommodation without even a farewell kiss to remember him by. And hadn't that bit hurt the most of all, even though she'd tried to convince herself it didn't matter? He'd been deep inside her body in the most intimate of ways and that didn't even warrant a goodnight kiss.

She'd spent the rest of the night tossing and turning in her narrow bed, unable to get rid of the memory of Leon as he had ridden her to fulfilment. She kept remembering the way she had cried out in rapture. She'd lain there in the claustrophobic staff accommodation, beating herself up about her behaviour—until the morning light had helped her put things in perspective.

She had been foolish and impulsive in a way which was totally out of character, that was all. She'd been living on her nerves since Pansy's arrest and maybe it was inevitable that sooner or later something was bound to give. But she hadn't hurt anyone—except perhaps herself—and she was going to draw a very firm line under the whole episode. The sex had been amazing—she wasn't going to deny that—but it wasn't going to lead anywhere. She was never going to see Leon again—he'd made it perfectly clear he didn't want to, and she had pretended she felt the same. And even though she had just been saving face, it was probably a good thing they *weren't* on schedule for a repeat performance. Because Leon Kanonidou had made her feel...*vulnerable*, and vulnerability had no place in her life. Didn't she have enough on her plate, without pining after some boho biker who probably slept with a different woman every night of the week?

She could feel her cheeks growing hot as she met Jodie's curious stare. 'I just didn't sleep very well last night,' she said truthfully. 'I think a mosquito must have got into the room because every time I closed my eyes I could hear that awful high-pitched whining sound buzzing around the room.'

Jodie shuddered. 'Tell me about it. I hate

mosquitos. Get some of the spray they sell in the hotel shop—the one with the red label. I know it's expensive but it works wonders.'

'I will. Though I'm not sure it's great for the lungs. Anyway—' Marnie forced a smile '—who's this manicure for?'

Her nails glinting coral in the bright Greek sunshine, Jodie glanced down at her clipboard. 'One of the women in that party who've taken over the western side of the hotel. You know—the billionaire who's having the birthday celebrations. Her name is Ariane Paparizou and she's requested a mini manicure. Poolside.'

'And when does she want it?'

'Are you kidding me?' Jodie pulled a comic face. 'Like *yesterday*? You know what these wealthy women are like.'

Marnie nodded. She certainly did. A few seemed like perfectly decent people but many of them were spoiled and, in her experience, nearly all of them were demanding. So she tidied her hair, checked her portable nail kit and then made her way through the sprawling Paradeisos complex towards the upmarket Ouranos section. She'd never actually done a treatment here before—Jodie usually kept the jobs with the greatest tip potential for herself—and ordinarily Marnie might have been excited at the thought of having a peek round this most exclusive area of the hotel. But today didn't feel ordinary. Not at all. She still had that strange feeling of being disconnected from her own body. As if being given two orgasms in quick succession by a man she barely knew had shaken the foundations of her world and made her realise she didn't really know herself very well at all.

Abundant pink and white flowers framed the interconnecting buildings surrounding the different-sized swimming pools which made the Ouranos complex so distinct, though naturally it had its own private beach. It was just unfortunate that the thought of any kind of beach made Marnie want to shudder. It made her think of grains of sand falling onto the floor of her tiny shower cubicle and swirling down the plughole as she'd tried to wash away the memories of Leon's lovemaking. But his scent had clung stubbornly to her hair and her skin and it had taken a full twenty minutes of fierce scrubbing before she'd finally felt free of him and able to fall into bed last night.

She could hear the chink of glasses and as she approached, her gaze took in the kind of scene which looked like an advertiser's dream. Around a vast azure pool stood a cluster of rich and beautiful people—all speaking in Greek and laughing while waiters topped up their crystal goblets with champagne. Several of the women lay sprawled on sun loungers and they were all wearing tiny scraps of swimwear which looked hugely expensive. But that was because they were. Marnie had seen the discreet price tags in the hotel boutique and marvelled at the fact that anyone would ever spend that much on a bikini.

From beneath the wide brim of her straw hat, one of the women spotted her and lifted her hand in careless greeting. 'Ah! My manicurist is here. At last!' she exclaimed, in perfect if slightly dramatic English. 'Never has the sight of someone been so welcome!'

Everyone turned to stare at her, their voices growing silent as Marnie walked towards the group. Finding herself the unwilling focus of attention made it difficult to avoid becoming self-conscious as she moved across the terrace. She was dimly aware of the women's collective beauty and that the men were all tall and devastatingly handsome. But her unease quickly became acute as the identity of one of the guests seared itself onto her disbelieving brain and at first she thought it must be some sort of mirage. *Please, no,* she thought. *Please don't do this to me.* She could feel the savage pounding of her heart as she risked a glance towards the most captivating member of the group and could see that her prayers hadn't been answered.

Because it was Leon.

Leon the biker, who'd picked her up on the beach.

Lion-like Leon, to whom she'd given her virginity.

But this Leon looked nothing like the man she'd kissed so passionately last night while his fingers had been playing a rhapsody between her legs. Today there were no faded denims. No close-fitting black T which caressed his ripped torso—and definitely no sign of a dusty old motorbike. He wore an expensive linen shirt, unbuttoned at the neck, and navy swim shorts. His black hair was tamed and sleek, not windswept and ruffled. He was looking cool and immaculate, yes—but his head-turning qualities were due to much more than his rugged good looks and muscular body, for he radiated power and privilege in the way that only the truly wealthy ever could. Marnie wanted to look away but somehow she couldn't. She was mesmerised by those eyes which rivalled the sky behind him, for they were dominating her line of vision and burning into her like blue fire. Was his expression mocking her, she wondered, or was he just acutely embarrassed to see her here?

Awkwardly, she moved towards the woman who was beckoning her with a rather impatient finger, and realised that if she didn't get it together, she would start stockpiling complaints about her lack of professionalism—and that was the last thing she could afford to happen. But the efficient smile she was usually able to summon up at will for clients seemed to have deserted her. 'Ariane Paparizou?' she croaked.

'That's me! Don't just stand there. Come and sit down.' Ariane turned her head with a swish of a glossy black ponytail and flashed the onlookers a wide smile. 'I'm sure the others don't mind watching while…what's your name, dear?'

'Marnie.'

'While Marnie works her magic on me!' A small chair beside the lounger was patted and Marnie padded her way over to it, wishing the ground would open up and swallow her. Wishing she'd never met him. Wishing she were anywhere other than here. Taking the colour swatch of varnishes from her little bag, she splayed it out for Ariane's attention, but her head was buzzing with questions which seemed impossible to answer.

Like, *what was he doing here*? He was supposed to be a builder, wasn't he? Yet he was standing fraternising with these privileged people as if he had every right to be here and, judging from their fawning body language—he did. Suddenly, she realised that, whoever he was, he wasn't the man he had appeared to be—and that she had made a very bad choice for her first lover. Not just that, but she had been totally naïve—she, who always prided herself on being street-smart. She, the wisecracking victim of circumstance who was never going to allow herself to be conned by a smooth-talking man.

Of *course* he wasn't a builder! Yes, he'd been dressed in a laid-back way—but what else would he have been wearing if he'd been out in the hot sun all day, pelting around a Greek island on a motorbike in the height of summer? She remembered the restaurant where all the tables had supposedly been reserved…until Leon had appeared and one had

miraculously been made available by a proprietor who had been fawning over them all
evening. Would they have done that for an
ordinary builder? Of course they wouldn't!

Flicking him another glance, she could see
he was the only one not drinking champagne,
for he was holding a glass of water. His expression was dark and brooding and he was
still staring at her. Staring very hard. Any
minute now and someone might notice that
his attention was—inappropriately—fixed
on the visiting beautician and start to wonder
why. Or was she flattering herself? Were casual sexual games with staff members par for
the course for these kind of people?

Pulling out her kit bag, she began to rummage inside it but all she could think about
was that bright gaze which had burned itself
into her consciousness.

'Leon...'

Marnie almost dropped her cuticle-pusher
as Ariane said the name she had cried out
last night, and the little hairs on the back of
her neck stood to attention as she heard his
murmured response.

'Mmm?'

'Would you like to help me choose a colour?'

There was a pause. 'Nail polish isn't really my area of expertise I'm afraid, Ariane.'

Sweat began to bead on Marnie's brow as she found herself thinking the unthinkable. *Because what if Ariane and Leon were lovers and he'd taken a few hours out to be unfaithful to her last night?* It was a grim possibility but it was still a possibility and, in the sort of world in which she'd grown up, it remained a very real one.

'Marnie?'

Ariane's voice broke into her thoughts and Marnie felt another trickle of fear sliding down the back of her neck. What if the gorgeous Greek woman knew exactly what had happened? Maybe they'd even discussed it and laughed about it—in a very modern way? *I know I shouldn't have done it, agape mou, but she kind of threw herself at me.*

She swallowed. What if Ariane called the hotel management and dobbed her in for being intimate with one of the guests—something which was strictly forbidden? What if she was sent home in disgrace with a black mark on her CV and, much more importantly, without the inflated bonus she had been relying on to help her twin sister when she got out of prison?

'Y-yes?' Marnie questioned, her cheeks burning with dread.

'I'll have the Early Sunrise, please.'

Marnie blinked as Ariane jabbed her broken fingernail in the direction of a vivid orangey hue, and she stared at it as if she had never seen that particular shade of varnish before. 'Yes, yes. Of course. A...a very good choice. It's been very popular with all our clients this summer.' She flashed a smile. 'Is there somewhere I can go to fill up my nail bath?'

Ariane flicked a hand in the direction of one of the sleek white buildings. 'There's a bathroom in there—first on the left. You can't miss it.'

As Marnie began to walk across the sunlit patio, Léon couldn't tear his gaze away from her because right now she seemed like the personification of his perfect dream.

Or his perfect nightmare.

He was having difficulty breathing. Difficulty thinking of anything other than the way she had wrapped her legs around his back last night while he had thrust deep into her virgin tightness. Had he thought he would never run into her again? Yes—and a million times yes. Because that was for the best. He was all wrong for her and she was definitely all wrong for him. Not just because she was unsophisticated and innocent and would never have fitted into his world—nor he into hers—but because he didn't recognise the man he had become in her company.

Wild—tick. Reckless—another tick. But it had been the way he had lost control which had so disturbed him. Or rather, the realisation that someone else had the power to take that control away from him which had bothered him most. As a child he had been manipulated by the subterfuge of his mother and the widespread influence of his father and at times had felt powerless. *That* was the feeling he'd been determined never to revisit but, last night, he had done just that—and it had scared him. He, who despised fear almost as much as he despised lies.

Which was why, when he had dropped Marnie off, he had resisted the urge to kiss her—despite the red-hot invitation of her lips. Just as he hadn't taken her back to her room and made love to her again, even though powerful desire had raged inside his body. He had forced himself to listen to the voice of reason and had said nothing but a terse goodnight as she slid from the back of his bike.

But now she was here and he knew he had to get her alone, though he didn't stop to ask himself why. Putting his glass down on a nearby table, he began to follow her into the shady interior of the villa. He could hear the sound of running water and there, in the open doorway of a bathroom, stood Marnie, bending over a sink. He saw her shoulders stiffening and her head jerking up, as if she'd sensed someone was behind her and that it was him. Was she as acutely aware of his presence as he was of hers, he wondered distractedly, even from this distance? But no, she was actually looking at him in the mirror and her furious expression was reflected back at him.

'Go away,' she snapped.

'I need to talk to you.'

'To say *what*?' Holding her little container of water, she turned to face him and her anger was far more intense when witnessed face-on, rather than through the cool barrier of the glass. 'To explain how you got invited to a fancy party like this? They don't look like the kind of people who would be hobnobbing with their builder, unless society is a lot more equal here than I thought it was. What happened, Leon—did you decide to leave your trowel and cement behind, or did I arrive too late to see you scaling up a ladder? Because you're not a builder at all, are you?'

'In a way, I am—'

'Please don't insult my intelligence by playing with words! You know exactly what I mean.'

Leon's mouth flattened. Her fury was delectable enough to make him want to smile, but he sensed the embarrassment behind the words she flung at him. 'There's a reason I didn't tell you.'

'I'm sure there is. And what might that be, I wonder?' Her gaze raked over his body, but it was a cold and damning assessment and nothing like the hungry gaze she had subjected him to over dinner last night. 'You're obviously a very rich man, Leon. I guess you need to hide that fact away from casual hook-ups, in case they start making demands on your wealth!'

'But I don't *do* casual hook-ups!'

'Really? So did I just dream what happened last night? Was it all a figment of my imagination?' There was the faintest, telltale wobble of her lips before she looked over his shoulder and her angry expression quickly morphed into a brisk and professional smile. 'Kyria Paparizou!' she gushed. 'I'm so *sorry* to have kept you—I was just running the water to get it to exactly the right temperature for your nails. Certainly. Yes, of course! I'll be right there!'

Leon was so taken aback by the unwanted interruption that he stepped aside to let her pass, tantalisingly aware of her scent before reluctantly turning and wondering how the persistent Ariane Paparizou was going to react when she saw him talking to the manicurist.

Until he realised that the Greek heiress was nowhere to be seen! Only Marnie herself, sashaying across the brilliant patio, with the white material of her uniform stretched alluringly over her buttocks and her hair a million different shades of gold. His body tensed. So, it had been nothing but a ruse to get her away from him—and he had fallen for it! He wasn't used to being wrong-footed and for a moment he just stood there, watching her retreat.

Suddenly she turned and flashed him a triumphant look—as if she was enjoying having outsmarted him—and Leon felt the corresponding stir of hunger in his blood. As she sat down on the stool to start working on Ariane's nails, he walked out onto the terrace.

A waiter handed him a drink and he knew

he ought to join one of the small clusters of people who were laughing and drinking beneath the shade of big white umbrellas. But all he wanted to do was to stare at Marnie and drink in the way the sunlight was gleaming on her bare legs. Last night he had been determined he wasn't going to see her again—but in the bright light of day, that suddenly didn't seem like such a good idea.

'So, Leon. This is where you're hiding.'

A male voice shattered his contemplation and Leon glanced across at the man who had joined him—Xenon Zafiris, heir to a massive shipping line. The two men had moved in similar circles when they'd been teenagers but had never really been friends.

He flicked Xenon a cool smile. 'As you see, I'm in plain sight.'

'So you are. How was America?'

'Oh, you know. Big.'

'And England?'

'Pretty small.'

'I hear you've been doing stuff in Northern Greece.' Xenon raised his eyebrows. 'Drilling for wells, on a no-profit basis.'

'That's right.' Leon's voice became thoughtful. 'The land up there badly needs water. There's no limit to the possibilities for future farming, if we just get the irrigation right.'

'Philanthropy is always such an admirable trait,' observed Xenon softly, before curving his lips into a smile. 'But on a more personal level… I gather your father is getting married again. Are you planning to attend the wedding?'

'I'm sure I'll be able to fit it in,' answered Leon, with a shrug.

There was a pause. 'Which number is that, I wonder? It's so easy to lose count.'

'Four, I believe.' Leon's voice was dismissive, because he didn't want to talk about his father, or his wives, or to inform a man whose imagination was so limited that he used his leisure time to gossip. He wanted to be left alone to study Marnie Porter, even though she had just slanted him a look of pure ice. He took a sip of water to ease the dryness in his throat. Was he discovering a previously unknown streak of masochism? he wondered wryly. No woman had ever looked at him that way before and his pulse was pounding like a piston in response.

'Easy on the eye, isn't she?' said Xenon, following the direction of his gaze. 'Though I can't quite work out what the attraction is.

I mean, she's wearing a pretty unflattering uniform and those rubber-heeled shoes make her look a bit like a nurse, and yet...'

Leon's body stiffened as Xenon's speculative observation died away. He knew that men often discussed a woman's appearance, in the same way you might admire an amazing sunset or a good wine. His friends' wives told him that women sometimes did the same. It was no big deal and in many cases it wasn't even predatory. But this felt predatory and suddenly he felt the build-up of something unfamiliar. A slow, simmering rage that the renowned playboy Zafiris should dare to look at *his* lover in such a way.

But Leon didn't *do* jealousy. His eyes narrowed. Just as he didn't do commitment.

Or trust.

In fact, there was a whole list of no-go areas in his life, which helped shore up his determination never to get married, or have children.

Yet Marnie Porter had managed to achieve something which no other woman had succeeded in doing before, because there had been no need. She had turned him into a hunter.

Yet women usually came to *him*. They

flocked to him like wasps to honey. They didn't freeze him out with withering looks which seemed genuine rather than fabricated.

So why was his blood pulsing with the hottest desire he could ever remember?

He frowned.

What did the little hairdresser from Acton have which so entranced him?

CHAPTER FIVE

THE KNOCK ON the door was quiet yet insistent, but Marnie ignored it. She didn't want to see anyone and she *definitely* didn't want to speak to anyone. The hurt and humiliation she'd felt when she'd seen Leon Kanonidou down by the poolside with all his sophisticated buddies had been bad enough but she probably could have coped with it. Of course she could, because didn't it only reinforce what she had already known? That she could trust nobody. Nobody at all. The only person she could rely on was herself and she should forget that at her peril.

She had gone through the rest of the day on autopilot and returned to her room in time to receive a call from her twin in England—a short and deeply upsetting exchange before Pansy's prison phone credit ran out, which it always did. But the gist of the conversation had been devastating. Her twin's lawyer had announced that she probably *was* looking at a jail sentence and Marnie had listened to her sister's rising hysteria, feeling impotent and useless and too far away.

It had been the final straw and she had given into a violent flurry of tears which had taken her by surprise, because crying was something she rarely succumbed to. Had her sexual awakening made her more susceptible to the great swings of emotion which were barrelling through her and if that were the case, then wasn't that yet another reason to steer clear of men in future? Her sobs had subsided now and she had scrubbed at her face with a hankie, but someone knocking on her door was the last thing she wanted.

She didn't *care* if it was Jodie calling to see if she was feeling better, or one of the hotel waitresses enquiring whether she'd be interested in going out for a drink later, which she never was. Basically, she just wanted to tick off the hours until she could fly back to London and discover for herself if Pansy's lawyer was as bad as her sister claimed. And she would prefer to do it by burying her head underneath a duvet, and sleeping through the next twenty-four hours.

But it was only six in the evening and there was no duvet to be seen since, according to the hotel guidebook, the temperature on Paramenios was always warm—even in winter. And now, at the tail end of summer, it was almost unbearably hot in this cramped little room—with the noisy fan whirring away in one corner a poor substitute for air conditioning. And somehow she couldn't escape from the taunting memories which seemed determined to plague her.

Pushing a clump of hair away from her sticky brow, she remembered Leon watching while she painted the glamorous Ariane's nails. His gaze had been unsettlingly intense, as if he were examining her underneath a microscope, and she had felt...

No. She didn't really want to think about how she had felt—because it wasn't very helpful to realise that he had the ability to make her react in a way which was reminiscent of a helpless turtle which had just had the shell ripped from its back. She didn't want to dwell on her rush of mortification either, when Ariane had pressed a large banknote into her hand as a tip. Obviously, the money would come in very useful, but the ultra-generous amount had made her feel awkward—

and Marnie had only just stopped herself from declaring that she didn't need it.

As if.

But as she had scuttled away from that glittering group of revellers, she had felt *less than*. Just as she'd felt throughout most of her life. An outsider. The odd one out. The object of ridicule and scorn.

The knock was repeated.

'Will you go *away*?' she said. But the caller was nothing if not persistent, so eventually Marnie got up from the lumpy mattress and opened the door—her heart clenching like a vice when she saw Leon standing there. He had changed from his pool attire into a pair of tailored trousers and a charcoal-coloured shirt, which emphasised the blackness of his hair. These clothes were also screamingly expensive and hugged his muscular frame as if they'd been designed for him—which they probably had—and once again he seemed to represent a personification of virile power.

His unexpected appearance was a massive shock to the system but not as unwelcome as it should have been and instantly Marnie could feel her body begin to betray her again. Beneath the uniform dress, which she hadn't bothered to remove, she could feel her breasts springing into rampant life.

What was the *matter* with her? she wondered furiously. Why was she still attracted to such a deceiving cheat? Yet it horrified her to realise she was also worrying about how awful she must look, with her tear-streaked face and bedhead hair. Her hand tightened on the door handle as she tried not to think about the way he had kissed her. Tried to forget the hard warmth of his body and the way his fingers had stroked over her skin as her yelps of pleasure had subsided into purring little sighs. 'Go away right now or I'll slam the door in your face,' she vowed softly. 'And don't think I won't.'

'Are you sure you want to do that, Marnie?'

'Nothing would give me greater pleasure!'

'I would have to disagree with you on that particular point,' he remarked coolly and she blushed at the implication.

'Do you really think trying to ignore me is the best way to deal with our predicament?' he continued.

'The only *predicament* we have, Leon,' she echoed sarcastically, 'is two strangers standing looking at one another, with one of them wishing they'd never met.'

'So would that be you, I wonder, *agape mou*? Or me?'

'*Oh!*' she said, as wrong-footed by his silken retort as by his use of the word he'd murmured against her neck last night just before he'd made his fateful discovery of her innocence. But she didn't want to think about that either. She wanted to remind herself that he was trespassing and she had the upper hand. 'I'm not going to say it again,' she vowed.

'Five minutes. That's all.'

'And then you'll go?'

He shrugged. 'If you still want me to.'

He sounded so sure of himself, she thought furiously. So completely certain that she would comply with his wishes. She supposed the subtext was that no woman in her right mind would ever eject a man like him from the premises. Which was exactly what she *should* do. But his gaze was so steady and compelling and once again he was managing to exude an aura of power so spellbinding that, stupidly, she didn't want him to go. At least, not yet. Surely it wouldn't hurt to hear him out, especially as they had been so intimate. Because what if someone saw him and worked out what he was doing on her doorstep? Hadn't one of the waitresses recently been sacked for skinny-dipping with one of the clientele? She mustn't forget that she was leaving the day after tomorrow—so why jeopardise her much-needed bonus, by risking someone discovering she'd had sex with one of the hotel's most important guests?

She opened the door a little wider. 'I suppose you'd better come in,' she said.

'Efharisto.'

'I'd like to say *you're welcome*, but I'm not that much of a hypocrite!'

He smiled and instantly his powerful body seemed to suck up all the available light and air, as if the universe were silently acknowledging his formidable presence. Clicking the door shut, Marnie moved as far away from him as possible—not terribly easy in this confined space—because close up he was making her feel helpless. And she wasn't helpless. That was what she needed to remember. She was strong. That was her trademark. Her legacy from having been ejected from her mother's womb a full five minutes before her sister, and then left to deal with the dreadful fallout of that day. She tilted her chin and regarded him unwaveringly.

'Okay. You've got five minutes, and the clock is ticking.'

He didn't seem in the least bit fazed by her attitude—in fact, he was behaving as if he was enjoying the challenge rather than being annoyed by it. And didn't his unflustered air only add to his lazy confidence, which had been one of the things which had attracted her to him in the first place?

'You're angry,' he mused.

'Yes, I'm angry. But I'll get over it.'

'And you've been crying.'

'So? That's not a crime, is it?'

'Is it because I didn't ask to see you again?'

'Oh, the arrogance! Is that what you really think? That I've been sobbing into my pillow because you made clear it wasn't going to happen again?' She gave what she hoped was a liberated smile instead of the bitter laugh which was hovering on her lips. 'I may not have had much experience with men, but I've listened to enough people over the years to understand the meaning of a casual hook-up. Don't worry about it, Leon. I certainly wasn't expecting a repeat performance.'

'So what's the problem?'

Her smile vanished as quickly as it had appeared. The problem was that she felt overwhelmed by all her emotions—concern for her sister in prison but also how to deal with him. She'd been hurt before—many times—but never by a man, because she'd never put herself into a position where that could happen. And none of her usual coping mechanisms seemed to be working. She could admit that she'd found it humiliating to rock up with her manicure kit while he was standing quaffing champagne with his billionaire mates, but that wasn't really what all this was about.

'I thought you were like me,' she said.

He frowned. 'In what way?'

'Ordinary.' The word puffed out of her mouth. 'Not…'

'Rich?' he prompted, into the pause which followed.

'*Rich?*' she echoed. 'Oh, come on, Leon. I suspect that's a pretty modest assessment, judging by the bar bill which your party apparently ran up at lunch time, and by the way all the hotel staff keep referring to you all as if you're some kind of royalty.' She shook her head. 'Why didn't you tell me you were staying here when you dropped me off last night, instead of letting me run across you while I was working? I felt completely disoriented when I saw you down by the pool.'

'If you must know, I felt pretty disoriented myself.'

'My heart bleeds for you.'

'It doesn't show,' he said softly, his gaze flicking to the bodice of her white dress.

'Someone in the spa was talking about you just before I finished my shift earlier,' she said, wishing he wouldn't look at her that way. Wishing he'd pull her into his arms and kiss her as she wanted to be kissed. She swallowed in an attempt to dissolve the erotic image. 'And that's when I discovered how inaccurately you had described yourself. Because you're not a *builder*, are you, Leon? You're one of the biggest property developers around. One of the richest men in the world apparently.'

'I don't deny it.' He shrugged. 'Perhaps now you can understand why I didn't tell you.'

'Actually, I don't. So why don't you enlighten me?'

Leon's eyes narrowed. Did she really need him to spell it out? Usually, he would have sidestepped her questions because analysis was something he avoided whenever possible. But as he stared into her defiant face he honestly thought he would answer anything she asked of him right then. Was it her innate impishness, or the memory of her tight body which made him unusually indulgent with her? 'The Kanonidou name carries a lot of baggage,' he said heavily. 'And a lot of expectations.'

'And, *what*? Did you imagine I'd be trying to extract some of your fortune if I'd had any idea how rich you were? Demanding to know why you hadn't used a gold-plated pair of tweezers to remove the sea-urchin spines?'

'Do tweezers actually come in gold plate?'

'I expect so,' she said, pursing her lips as if she were trying not to laugh. 'You can get pretty much anything you want if the price is right.'

'You think I don't know that?' he demanded. 'For once in my life I was enjoying the fact that you didn't know who I was, or what I was worth, or what the papers are saying about my family. I can't remember the last time that happened.' He paused. 'And I've never had dinner with a woman who offered to split the bill before.'

The look on her face became proud—the light in her eyes very bright.

'I've always paid my way!' she declared. 'And it wouldn't have made the slightest bit

of difference if I'd known how much you had
in your bank account, because I don't care.
That wasn't the reason I had sex with you.'

'I know, that was what was different for
me. But I'm confused—what was the reason,
then? Because that's the bit that puzzles me,
Marnie. For most women their virginity is a
big deal. Why give your innocence to someone you've only just met?'

As he stared her down Marnie realised she
had backed herself into a corner. Naturally,
she was reluctant to admit how special he'd
made her feel because it was, well…irrele-
vant. It would make her appear needy—as
if nobody else had ever made her feel so desired, which also happened to be true. *And*
it would undoubtedly feed his ego, which
seemed inflated enough already. Yet if all
the things she'd heard were correct, sex was
mostly about the *physical* not the emotional,
especially where men were concerned.

So what was wrong with identifying with
that part of the equation?

Who wasn't to say that, when she got back
to England and managed to sort out Pansy's
current problems, she might actually find
herself a permanent boyfriend? Someone
more on her own wavelength. An ordinary

man with an ordinary job, not some unreachable Greek tycoon with the face of a fallen angel. And if that were the case, then surely it would be better to be a little bit experienced. Men had always made her super-cautious but now she'd lost her virginity—and, given how much she'd enjoyed it, why shouldn't she explore her own sexuality a little? Leon Kanonidou had asked her a straightforward question, so why not give him a straightforward answer?

'Because I wanted to,' she said bluntly. 'I wanted to forget the outside world and everything which was going on in my life and somehow you made me...' She shrugged. 'You made me...'

'I made you, what?'

The air seemed to grow very still. 'Desire you,' she breathed, her words sounding deliberate, and heavy.

'Wow.' His shuttered gaze made his eyes resemble splinters of sapphire as he breathed out his reaction. 'That's quite some testimony.'

'You aren't used to women praising your prowess?'

'Not like that.'

'Well, I give you full permission to use it

on your CV,' she said flippantly. 'But I'd prefer the source to remain anonymous, if it's all the same to you.'

'I'll bear that in mind,' he said, and gave a low growl of laughter.

The sound was rich and sexy but Marnie forced herself to remember that it meant nothing. It was an illusion. She'd just made a powerful man laugh—so what? Nothing had changed. He was still a billionaire who had preferred to keep his identity private in case she started muscling in on his wealth, and she was still a tear-stained misfit standing in an overheated room, due to go back to England where a mountain of problems awaited her.

'So now you know and you can go,' she said quietly.

'But I don't know. Your explanation has only thrown up more questions.' He stood there like a dark and immovable force, his eyes glittering as they stared her down. 'And now I'm curious to know what was going on in your life which you so badly wanted to forget.'

If only his words weren't softened with what sounded like genuine concern. Something which resembled *kindness*. Because that was Marnie's undoing. That was what made her defences begin to weaken. She curled her hands into two tight fists, her fight-or-flight instinct kicking into action. After a childhood of being let down so many times, she wasn't used to people being kind because she never let them close enough to try. The habit of a lifetime had taught her to guard her secrets and lock them away, because that was the safest thing to do.

But Leon Kanonidou knew her more intimately than anyone else. He had been deep inside her, his hard flesh united with hers so that for a while she had actually felt as if they were one person. Was it that which made her hesitate and foolishly give him the opening he was seeking?

'It's my…sister,' she said. 'My twin sister, Pansy. I've been worried about her, that's all.'

She recovered enough to follow this up with a dismissive nod, indicating that the subject was closed—but Leon Kanonidou was either oblivious to the hint or deliberately choosing to ignore it.

'What's happened to her?'

'I didn't say anything had happened to her.'

'But that's what you implied.' His gaze was very steady. 'Tell me.'

Was this how people got so powerful?

Marnie wondered wildly. Did they just use the compelling force of their personalities to make you feel you actually *wanted* to confide in them? Well, maybe Leon would get more than he bargained for. She couldn't imagine him hanging around to investigate further once he discovered the facts. 'She's in trouble with the law,' she said, the words sticking like glue to her throat.

'Why?'

She shook her head. 'It doesn't matter.'

'Tell me,' he said again.

Oh, but his voice was so soft, so deep, so cajoling. It lulled her into a false sense of security. It made her imagine—for one brief and shining moment—how it might feel to have someone you could lean on.

'She's always been a bad judge of men. Maybe it's congenital.' She gave a short laugh and had the pleasure of seeing him flinch. 'Her latest boyfriend asked her to carry a bag to Monaco for him and she agreed. I'm sure you can guess the rest.'

'Drugs?' he said quietly, his expression grim.

'Diamonds, actually.' But then Marnie stopped thinking about Leon—stopped thinking about anything other than lovely

Pansy, who should have known better, but who trusted people way more than she ever should. 'But she didn't know what was in it!' she burst out passionately. 'She honestly didn't know. You could rightly accuse her of being too gullible, but she's not a criminal. She's innocent!'

His blue eyes were very intense. 'That's what they all say.'

His cynical assessment made Marnie furious that she'd told him, and as angry tears sprang to her eyes she tried to turn away from him. But he stopped her. He put his hands on her shoulders and she could feel the power which flowed from their steady weight. And then he did the most unexpected thing. He reached one hand to her face to slowly wipe away the track of wetness which had trickled down her cheek. Somehow the gesture disarmed her and she couldn't afford to let it. She jerked away from him, aware and afraid of what his touch could do to her.

'Don't you dare judge her!'

'I'm not judging her,' he said. 'I'm just telling you how a prosecution lawyer would look at it.'

'Oh, so you're an expert in law as well, are you?'

'Let's just say I have a working knowledge of legal matters,' he answered drily. 'Where is she now?'

'In prison. In London.' She stared at him defiantly. 'There! Shocked?'

'It takes a lot to shock me, *agape*,' he demurred. 'Won't they grant her bail?'

She moved her shoulders uncomfortably, knowing that she had said too much, but something about his response made her want to continue—because hadn't she been bottling this up for so long? 'No,' she said flatly. 'No bail. They think she might be vulnerable to outside influence—which is probably true.'

'From the boyfriend?' he interjected.

She pulled a face. 'Yeah. The ex-boyfriend now. The case comes to court soon but the lawyer they've given her is rubbish. That's the reason I came to Greece. It's pretty much a certainty that Pansy's going to get a custodial sentence, so I took this job because it's unbelievably well paid and my salon in London gave me a leave of absence.' The words were bubbling out now. Bubbling out in a torrent she couldn't seem to stop. Yet wasn't it a relief to say this stuff out loud, instead of letting it join all the other dark secrets which hung heavy on her shoulders? 'At first I was determined to get her a better lawyer but when I discovered how much they charge per hour, I realised how naïve I was being. So instead I thought...'

Sapphire eyes speared into her. 'You thought what?'

She shook her head. 'It doesn't matter.'

'Marnie.' There was a pause. 'Please.'

It was a request but it was also a command and Marnie sucked in a breath, hating the way he seemed to be taking control. *Hating it, yet revelling in it all at the same time.* 'I thought I could save some money for her. So she'd have something to support herself with when she was set free. A nest-egg to get her started. At least that's something I *can* achieve.'

Leon watched as she fished a tissue from the pocket of her uniform and blew her nose, and afterwards surveyed him with an expression of defiance and vulnerability. He noted the untidy spill of her hair and the pinkness around her eyes and felt a tug of something he didn't recognise deep inside him.

'And what about your parents?' he said. 'Where do they come in all this? Can't they help?'

He saw her stiffen.

'My mother is dead and I never...' She

lifted her jaw almost pugnaciously. 'I never knew my father. So now you know. You've heard everything and you can go.' Her gaze was very steady. 'Can't you?'

All her defiance was still there but so too was a sudden sense of wariness which had made her words so brittle. Leon wondered if she was expecting condolences about her parents, but he made none. He couldn't be that hypocritical and, besides, wouldn't she be appalled if he told her the truth? That part of him envied her the inevitable freedom which resulted from being orphaned?

But she had painted a bleak picture of her life. Of someone struggling on her own and fighting against the odds. He looked around the small room, which was so hot it felt like being in a sauna. At the hairbrush lying on a table, next to a pile of well-read books and a photo of a beautiful woman who looked a lot like her. Was that her sister? A large, half-filled suitcase lay open on the floor in one corner and his gaze lingered on it for a moment longer. Did that mean she was leaving? And despite the inner voice of caution which was urging him to stay out of her troubles, he found himself ignoring it.

'I can help you,' he said suddenly.

Her suspicious eyes became iron-hard as she shook her head. 'I don't want your help.'

Leon frowned, for this was the last thing he had expected. In a world where wealth talked, he'd never met anyone who wasn't eager to have a conversation. People never refused his money or influence. But then, he'd never met anyone like Marnie Porter before and the fierce pride radiating from her tiny frame drew from him an unwilling sense of admiration. 'I have the wherewithal and the resources to help your sister,' he growled. 'Let me put them at your disposal.'

'Thank you for the offer. It's very kind of you and I appreciate it,' she said. 'But no.'

'Why not?'

She considered his question for a moment. 'Because I don't really know you,' she said at last. 'And I don't want to be beholden to you. I don't want to be beholden to anyone.'

He stared into her determined face and could see she meant it. But he could also see that she was far from immune to him.

Nor he to her.

Her eyes had grown dark and the way she was chewing on her bottom lip was failing to conceal its telltale tremble. Against the bodice of the white uniform dress he could see the tantalising thrust of her nipples as they silently acknowledged his proximity—just as the hard ache at his groin acknowledged hers. He could feel the throb of mutual desire which flowed between them like like some tangible life-force. The sexual chemistry between them had been intense and powerful from the start—and, oh, the temptation to capitalise on it was overwhelming.

He knew he could pull her into his arms and kiss her and within minutes she would be kissing him back with the same hunger which had captivated him on the beach last night. He swallowed, tortured by all the possibilities which might follow such a move. He pictured his hands exploring her newly awoken body, hearing those mewling little cries of hunger as she touched him back. He imagined his fingers rucking up her uniform dress to slide down panties he suspected would already be wet. Would she instinctively tilt her pelvis towards him—inviting him to ravish her here, where she stood, her back pressed up against the wall and her legs wrapped around his back? Or would she lead him over to that lumpy-looking bed where they could spend a long and sticky night together?

But that would be wrong, on so many levels. He needed an outspoken hairdresser with a sister in jail like he needed a hole in the head.

The aching in his body was almost unendurable but Leon forced himself to project an indifference which, for once, was proving elusive.

'If that's what you want.'

'It is.'

'Then I guess I must wish you well. Goodbye, Marnie.'

'Goodbye, Leon.'

He saw the shadow which flickered over her face just before he turned his back on her and wondered if she would break in the short time it took for him to walk to the door. Would she call him back and tell him she'd changed her mind? Tell him that she wanted his money *and* his body—and didn't the prospect of that fill him with heady anticipation?

But she didn't.

She didn't say another word as he let himself out into the sultry darkness of the Greek evening and Leon experienced a powerful sense of disappointment.

And surprise.

CHAPTER SIX

AMBER SUNLIGHT SLANTED in through the windows of the tiny London pub and although a TV screen was showing highlights of a hugely anticipated football match, most people were watching the bubbly blonde who was waving a half-empty champagne flute in the air.

'Ooh, I'm just so thrilled! I can't believe it, Marnie,' she was cooing. 'After all the dire predictions the court just *threw* the case out!'

Marnie shook her head and smiled. 'It's wonderful,' she breathed. 'And no, I can't quite believe it either.'

They were sitting in the nearest pub to the courthouse in central London, while her sister celebrated her acquittal in typical, flamboyant style. She was wearing a leopard-skin jacket over a very short black dress and her bottom-length blonde hair was accessorised with a glittering gold headband. It probably wasn't the best choice of clothing in which to attend an important court hearing and Marnie had been amazed at the eventual outcome. All charges against her sister had been quashed, the surprising verdict no doubt due to Pansy's slick new barrister who had defeated the prosecution lawyer with his clever arguments and was now joining them for a celebratory glass of prosecco.

Pansy's new barrister.

As the euphoria following the verdict began to evaporate, Marnie's buzzing mind started focussing on Walker Lapthorne, who had made a dramatic, eleventh-hour appearance at the beginning of the trial. A handsome and sophisticated lawyer who didn't come cheap. Marnie had looked up his rates soon after his unexpected appearance at the start of the case and had stared at them in disbelieving horror. Who on earth could afford to employ someone of his calibre? She remembered the panic which had flooded through her. What if Pansy had done something completely dumb—like taking out a bank loan to hire one of the country's best barristers to defend her? And why was she now batting her eyelashes at the russet-haired attorney as if she were completely smitten? Marnie had tried to get her sister alone ever since they'd sat down in the pub, but had met with a deliberate stonewalling by her twin, and a refusal to budge from Walker's side.

Well, there was nothing else for it but to ask the question out loud.

Marnie cleared her throat. 'Mr Lapthorne?'

'Walker, please.'

'Walker. Firstly, a great big thank you for helping my sister get the justice she deserves.'

The lawyer smiled. 'My pleasure.'

Marnie lowered her voice. 'I'm assuming you weren't appointed to be Pansy's lawyer through legal aid?'

He nodded, his expression growing slightly veiled. 'Your assumption is correct.'

'And I know she couldn't possibly afford to pay your fees.' Marnie fixed her twin with a questioning look. 'You didn't pay them, did you, Pan?'

'Of course I didn't,' spluttered her twin. 'How could I?'

Her innocence sounded genuine and Marnie found herself despairing at the way her sister had always operated. She had always closed her mind off to the unpleasant things in life if she suspected they might compromise her in some way. It was presumably why she had agreed to carry a bag which wasn't hers for a smooth-talking boyfriend. And if a mysterious lawyer had appeared out of the blue and informed her he was going to be her saviour, Pansy would simply have smiled and said yes, please.

But if Pansy hadn't paid for the services of Walker Lapthorne, then who had?

Briefly, Marnie closed her eyes as an unwanted image swam into her mind. Of a man with blue eyes which blazed like sapphires and a naked body bathed silver by the light of the stars.

He wouldn't.

Would he?

Not when she had expressly told him not to.

She forced herself to continue. 'So, who *did* employ you to take on this job, Mr Lapthorne?'

The lawyer's voice acquired a little edge. 'I'm really not at liberty to say, Miss Porter.'

Marnie nodded. She wanted to ask him more but acknowledged the finality in his tone. And anyway—if her suspicions were correct—how on earth could she explain away such a random and generous action on the part of the Greek tycoon? Would she honestly want Pansy to know the reason *why*

Leon had done it—or Walker, if he hadn't already guessed?

Repeating her congratulations, she rose to her feet, kissed her sister goodbye and let herself out of the pub, stepping into a flurry of leaves, their dark swirl controlled by an autumn wind which had suddenly grown biting. Although she had the rest of the day off, she was reluctant to go home just yet—not with all these unanswered questions swirling around in her head. She bought herself a takeaway coffee, carried it to one of the nearby garden squares and sat down on an iron bench.

It had to be Leon.

But Leon lived in Greece.

A wave of confusion washed over her. He hadn't actually told her that, had he? In fact, he had told her remarkably little about himself—something she could strongly identify with, but not in these particular circumstances.

Putting her coffee down, she took out her phone and tapped his name into the search engine and there it was. Thousands of entries about the Kanonidou empire, less so about the man himself. But several things became instantly apparent. That Leon had a home and a branch of his company in central London—*and he had flown into the capital just the week before*!

So it could have been him.

Who else would have done it?

Marnie's throat dried and her heart began to race. She needed to find out for sure and then to…to what? To thank him? Of course she was grateful—hugely grateful—but she couldn't quite shake off her air of suspicion. She'd never met anyone who did something for nothing—which made her wonder just *why* he had done it.

But these thoughts were nothing but self-indulgence. If her hunch was correct then Leon had been unbelievably generous towards her sister and she needed to tell him that. What was she so afraid of? But she knew that, too. She was scared of the way he made her feel. Scared of the things he made her want. She'd been thinking of little other than him since she'd flown back from Greece and touched down at a rainy Stansted airport. Hadn't she returned to work at the salon unable to stop fixating on him, causing a couple of her colleagues to remark that she had been unusually quiet and preoccupied? And they had been right.

She focussed her search on the whereabouts of his London offices and discovered they were in Mayfair, not far from Bond Street Tube station. Soon she was standing outside a small, modern block of offices which sat comfortably beside the imposing splendour of its eighteenth-century neighbours.

As she headed towards a discreet smoked glass door bearing the Kanonidou name, Marnie felt a sudden onset of nerves. Couldn't she have sent him a thank-you card, or a bottle of whisky in a flashy wooden box? She found herself wondering if she was using his interference as an excuse to see him again and whether this was the start of a slippery slope which was only ever going to lead downwards.

Her mind kept returning to their last meeting, when she'd told him about Pansy and had refused the help he'd offered. She remembered feeling empowered as she had announced that she didn't want to be beholden to anyone. *But he had ridden roughshod over her wishes and done it anyway, hadn't he? What kind of arrogance was that?*

She remembered the terrible, sweet tension which had sizzled between them, with her alternately praying he would kiss her, then praying he wouldn't. And he hadn't. He had walked away without a backward glance and that had made her feel dark and lonely inside, her stomach twisted into knots of regret and rejection.

She caught a glance of herself reflected back in the glass of the Kanonidou building. The wind had managed to free some of the hair which she had coiled into a sensible updo for the court hearing, and the sober charcoal suit she had hoped would reflect well on her wayward sister made her look as if she were moonlighting as a bailiff. But she wasn't here because she wanted to appear attractive to the Greek billionaire. She was here to say her thanks, and then leave.

What if he wasn't here?

Well, it was too late to change her mind because a revolving door was expelling her into a huge reception area, filled with jungle-like foliage, and Marnie felt as out of place as she'd ever felt—especially when she noticed a uniformed security guard studying her from between narrowed eyes. A beautiful brunette behind a wide desk was sending a questioning look in her direction, the angle of her jaw suggesting that Marnie had no right to be here.

But she did.

She most certainly did.

Trying not to feel overwhelmed by the cavernous dimensions of the place, she made her way to the desk—fixing her face with the determined expression she'd used with social workers during most of her turbulent childhood.

'I'd like to see Leon Kanonidou, please,' she said.

'I'm afraid Mr Kanonidou doesn't see anyone without an appointment.'

'How do you know I haven't got an appointment?'

The brunette gave a serene smile. 'Because I have his diary sitting right in front of me and your name isn't on it.'

'But you don't know my name.'

'No, but I do know all the people on his list and you aren't among them.'

Marnie chewed on her lip. In a way she admired the woman's resolve, which was easily a match with her own—but if this receptionist thought she was going to slink away from here with her tail between her legs, then she thought wrong.

'Tell him Marnie Porter is here,' she said quietly. 'He'll see me.'

It was amazing how many insecurities

you could hide behind a mask of bravado, but for once in her life Marnie was sure of herself, confident that Leon *would* see her. Because wasn't there something powerful which pulled her to him and vice versa? Some unseen force which flowed between them—as strong as molten metal. Wasn't it that same force which had made him hire an expensive lawyer to get her sister out of a fix? Which had brought her here today, even though every atom of her body was telling her it was dangerous.

The receptionist's perfect brow pleated into a frown as she picked up a phone and had a brief conversation which resulted in her giving a grudging nod. But any triumph Marnie felt at having got her own way was short-lived, because the realisation that she was actually going to face Leon again was making her feel dizzy. Would she have gained some kind of immunity to him by now? Would she be able to look at him without wanting him to pin her down onto the nearest horizonal surface?

As a flash elevator swished her upwards, she wished she'd had the good sense to use a bathroom to repair her wayward hair and perhaps apply a slick of lipstick. She had already decided she didn't particularly care about impressing him, but she didn't want to come over as looking a total mess. But the elevator doors were sliding open and another gorgeous brunette was waiting outside. Did he order them from a catalogue? she wondered. This one was dressed in a neat black pencil skirt, a pristine white silk shirt and vertiginous black heels.

'Miss Porter?' the woman questioned.

Marnie nodded. 'That's me. I've come to see Leon.'

'If you'd like to come this way. Kyrios Kanonidou is expecting you.'

No time for second thoughts, just time to breathe deeply in a vain attempt to calm the wild thunder of her heart—while Marnie followed the black pencil skirt over a softly carpeted floor and into a vast office, whose windows overlooked the carefully tended grass of Hanover Square.

A lifetime of being summoned into alien offices had honed her ability to take a rapid measure of the tycoon's inner lair and, naturally, it was impressive. Spectacular paintings covered the walls, making it far less impersonal than most offices. There were big windows with amazing views and an even bigger desk, on which she could see a fancy cream card edged in gleaming gold, which looked like an invitation.

And then she noticed Leon standing on the other side of the room, watching her—the faintest of curves tilting his hard mouth into an ironic smile. As if he were used to being the first thing someone looked at, not the last. What did his expression tell her? Was that bemusement she could read? It was difficult to tell. She blinked, trying to adjust her eyes to the bright light—trying to get her head around the fact that this was the man who had kissed her, and held her. Who had taken her virginity with a consummate skill which had made her want to weep with disbelieving joy.

Yet today he looked like a stranger in his smart city clothes. An intimate stranger in a dark suit and a sapphire tie which echoed his spectacular eyes. She felt poleaxed by his presence, aware of her stinging breasts, which had started rubbing against her bra, and the rush of syrupy heat to her panties. It was as if her body were acknowledging him with ecstatic familiarity, even if her mind remained deeply mistrustful. She had certainly not acquired any desired immunity, she realised, too late.

'Marnie,' he said, his rich voice caressing her skin like velvet. 'This is an unexpected surprise.'

'Is it really?' she questioned quietly and when he didn't answer, she continued. 'Did you pay for my sister's defence lawyer, Leon?'

His eyes narrowed. 'Did Walker tell you?'

She shook her head. 'He didn't break any confidentiality clause, if that's what you mean.'

'Then how did you find out?'

'I guessed it was you. Who else could it have been?'

He met her gaze. 'My actions were intended to be anonymous.'

'But you must have known I would try to find out.'

'Your powers of detection weren't my primary concern at the time, Marnie,' he said drily.

She flushed. 'No, of course not.'

He stared at her, eyebrows raised. 'So?'

'I came here to…to thank you. And to ask…' She swallowed before the words came tumbling out in a rush. 'To ask why you did it.'

The sigh Leon had been holding back left his lips at last because here came the infernal conundrum. Why *had* he done it? He had admired Marnie's passionate defence of her sister and her total belief in her innocence, that was for sure. The matter had been none of his business and she had told him to stay out of it, yet he despised unfairness and knew how situations could be weighted against you because of prejudice, or because you didn't have enough money to fight your corner.

But his interjection had been motivated by factors other than sympathy and the ability to help, and one of those had been a deep and lingering frustration. Had he subconsciously envisaged this very scenario, that she would come to him like this? Yes, he had. Of course he had. Initially, he'd thought that out of sight would be out of mind and he would quickly forget the feisty little blonde. It had been both irritating and perplexing to discover that hadn't been the case at all, and that he'd been thinking about her far more than was necessary. In fact, he'd been thinking about her a lot.

Maybe it was because Marnie Porter had given him a glimpse into a different kind of world—the kind he wasn't familiar with. One where the odds were stacked up against you if you happened to be poor. His own upbringing had been far from perfect but it had always been affluent. He'd always had the best that money could buy. And yet that made no difference. Money didn't make you happy.

His mouth hardened.

Wasn't he the living proof of that?

He watched as she readjusted the strap of her shoulder bag and thought how uncomfortable she looked in her 'smart' clothes. Yet, ironically, the badly cut jacket and skirt somehow managed to tantalise him. Was it because they hinted at the delicious flesh he knew lay beneath, rather than clinging to her voluptuous frame and announcing it to the world? Had bedding a virgin turned him into a latter-day prude? he wondered wryly.

'I did it because of what you told me,' he explained slowly. 'Your anger at your sister's imprisonment was very…affecting. As was your belief in her innocence. I don't like injustice and I was in a position to do something about it. So I did.'

'Just like that?' she said faintly.

He shrugged. 'Walker is a top-class lawyer who has done some brilliant work over the years. I had him take a look at your sister's case and he concurred that she was likely to be given a custodial sentence. So I asked if he would investigate further and he agreed. He went to see her in jail, believed in her innocence and then took her on as his client. You know the rest.'

She fixed that grey gaze on him, fierce and unwavering. 'Even though I'd explicitly said I didn't want to be beholden to you?'

'But you aren't,' he objected. 'Not in any way. If the money I paid to employ Walker is really bugging you, you can walk straight out of here, speak to one of my assistants and arrange to pay back the fees. Take as long as you like—a lifetime if you wish—I don't care. But we both know that would be a futile gesture because I don't need the money. I already have more than I know what to do with.'

'Then maybe you should try giving some away to charity!' she challenged.

'I already do.'

'And I suppose you consider me and my sister to be your latest charity?'

'Now there's a thought. What would we call it, I wonder?' he mused. 'The Proud Porter Charity?'

She pursed her lips in what looked like a disapproving gesture but a brief giggle escaped from them nonetheless, and Leon felt an unexpected flicker of achievement—as if he had done something remarkable by coaxing a smile from her. As if a man would have to work very hard to amuse this little hairdresser—and since he had never had to put in much effort for a woman before, the novelty value of that was also appealing. And didn't her smile kick-start his imagination? Didn't the soft curve of her lips plant a very graphic picture in his mind about on which particular part of his anatomy he'd like to feel them?

'Anyway,' she said, shifting a little awkwardly on a pair of extremely unflattering shoes. 'I've said thank you and I'm sure Pansy would echo that.'

'Shall we go and have a drink to toast her freedom?'

She regarded him suspiciously. 'When?'

He glanced at his watch. 'What about right now?'

'It's the middle of the afternoon!'

'So? Haven't you ever drunk champagne in the middle of the afternoon?'

The look on her face suggested she had not and, even though Leon was already doubting the wisdom of his invitation, he seemed powerless to stop himself from pursuing it.

'Come on, Marnie,' he continued softly. 'What do you have to lose?'

But she shook her head. 'Thanks, but no thanks. I have to get home and anyway, I'm not dressed to go for a drink.'

For a moment Leon was so surprised and yes, so *irritated* by her refusal that he was tempted to let her walk right out of that door. And then his gaze was drawn to the unwanted invitation to his father's wedding, which was lying in a prominent position on his desk, and he reminded himself that sometimes life's pleasures needed to be grabbed at.

'Then how about you let me give you a lift home instead?' he questioned evenly. 'To Act On.'

CHAPTER SEVEN

'WHAT DO YOU have to lose?' Leon had demanded when he'd invited her to toast her sister's freedom, and Marnie could have answered in an instant.

Her sanity?

Her composure?

Most of all, the sense that she still had some element of control over her life.

She had refused the drink and not just because she was wearing clothes which would have made her stand out like a sore thumb. It was more to do with the fact that Leon was such a big personality. He was so handsome and charismatic that people would be bound to stare at them if he took them to a fancy venue, which undoubtedly he would. What if people saw them together and started asking questions about her? It was a risk she wasn't prepared to take, having kept herself

below the radar all through her life. But Leon
was nothing if not persistent and eventually
Marnie had agreed to a lift home, thinking
he might send her off in a flashy car with a
chauffeur at the wheel. That part of the equation had been correct—she just hadn't been
expecting Leon to slide into the back seat beside her, his powerful presence immediately
dominating everything around him.

Despite the vast dimensions of the luxury
car, the atmosphere inside felt claustrophobic and not just because the windows were
tinted, concealing them from the outside
world. It was more to do with the realisation that she badly wanted him to touch her
again, even though every instinct was telling her that was a terrible idea. He was powerful and autocratic. He was right out of her
league. It was just a pity that her traitorous
body didn't seem to agree. Her palms were
sweaty. Her knees were trembling. Worst of
all, they were already snarled up in traffic and
Acton was a long way from the West End.
She swallowed, aware of the silken throb of
desire low in her belly. Would she be able to
endure another thirty minutes of this torture?
She wasn't sure.

'Shouldn't you be at work?' she demanded

when he crossed one long leg over another and she found herself following the movement like a dog eyeing the revolution of a can-opener.

'I'm the boss. My hours are my own and I can do whatever I like—within reason. What's the matter, Marnie?' he questioned softly, stilling her by putting his hand on her arm. 'You seem very fidgety.'

'Is it any wonder? I wasn't expecting company.'

'And is my company so very awful?'

'It's not that. It's more a case of... Leon! What...what the *hell* do you...' Her question tailed off as his thumb began to caress her through the thin material of her jacket and she wondered if he could feel her shiver. Just as she wondered how it was possible to feel so aroused when all he was stroking was her arm. '...do you think you're doing?' she whispered.

'I think you know perfectly well what I'm doing. I'm trying to find out whether your skin is as deliciously soft as I remember and it most certainly is.' Without missing a beat he moved his hand down to her leg. 'I'm also a little surprised to discover that you're wearing stockings, since you didn't strike me as a stockings kind of woman, Miss Porter.'

'What's that supposed to mean?'

'I thought you were prim.' A skim of fingertips against the quiver of flesh, as his voice deepened. 'And these don't feel remotely prim.'

His fingers were inching up beneath her skirt and Marnie knew now was not the moment to enlighten him that she found tights constricting and liked her skin to be able to breathe properly. She swallowed but that didn't affect the terrible dust-dry feeling in her throat. She knew she ought to slap his hand away and stop him, but the trouble was that she didn't *want* to stop him. She wanted his hand to continue creeping up towards its drenched and aching destination. Would it be so wrong to allow herself a few moments of bliss before telling him this was a bad idea, or could he then rightly accuse her of leading him on? But she was powerless to prevent her eyes from closing as he drew a light circle over one trembling thigh and she wondered if he'd noticed the spill of flesh over the top of her hold-ups.

But suddenly all her perceived imperfections didn't matter because his slow stroking was becoming more and more irresistible and it was taking all her willpower not to whimper her approval, especially since he had bent his head and begun trailing soft kisses across her neck.

'Leon,' she whispered, but that throaty murmur sounded nothing like her normal voice.

'Shh…'

His velvety cajolement made the words die on her lips because he had reached her panties at last and was pushing the moist fabric aside and her eyes snapped open in alarm.

'Your…driver,' she gasped.

'There's a screen between us and him,' he murmured. 'And it's one-way. He can't see us and he can't hear us.'

Afterwards Marnie would marvel at the fact that they'd been discussing the inner workings of a luxury car at such a moment, but right now she was busy having Leon kiss away her little cries of pleasure while his unseen fingers worked their magic. She told herself to call a halt to it before it was too late, but she didn't think there was anything on earth which would have given her the strength to do that. Her breasts were tingling. Her flesh was dissolving—that silken beat impossible to ignore—the pump of her blood gathering pace like a piston. And then she was coming. Coming hard against the pressure of his palm. Trying not to buck or to cry out, despite his reassurance about the privacy of the one-way screen. Her attempts to keep her orgasm secret seemed only to intensify the sensations which were pulsing through her. It was…incredible. It seemed to go on and on for ever.

Eventually, he withdrew his hand and she was aware of the faint smell of her sex in the air. In a daze her eyelids fluttered open to find Leon regarding her, a look of feral satisfaction on his face, a soft smile at his lips.

'Did you like that?' he questioned silkily.

'I hated every minute of it.' She hit the button of the electric window and it slid soundlessly down. 'Couldn't you tell?'

A rush of cold air swirled in and he laughed but that didn't quite disguise the shifting frustration on his features and Marnie boldly reached out to rub her fingers over the hardness which the expert cut of his expensive trousers was failing to hide. For a moment he groaned as she feathered her fingers up and down his rocky shaft, before firmly removing her hand and putting it on her lap.

'No,' he advised sternly.

'Don't you want to?' she questioned, confused.

'What do you think, Marnie? Of course I do. It just happens to be a slightly less discreet operation for men.'

'I wouldn't know,' she said sulkily.

'Neither would I.'

She turned to him, blinking very hard, unable to hide the surprise from her voice. Or the leap of pleasure in her heart. 'Are you saying—?'

'That I've never made a woman come on the back seat of my car? *Neh*, that's exactly what I'm saying,' he growled. 'Just like I've never had sex on a beach with someone I've only just met. I don't know what it is you do to me, Marnie Porter—only that I find I want you. I want you very badly.'

It was a heartfelt declaration and it startled her. A little flustered now, Marnie turned her head to stare out of the open window to see that Shepherd's Bush had come into view. They must have been in the car longer than she'd thought. Her heart began to race. What did they say about time passing quickly when you were having fun—and wasn't that the best fun she'd had in years?

She turned back to find him studying her. In the dim light his features were shadowed, making the brilliance of his eyes stand out like jewels. And suddenly she thought, why *shouldn't* they carry on what they'd just started? Mutual pleasure between two consenting adults wasn't any sort of crime, was it? Because yes, she'd just had the most amazing orgasm but Leon must be extremely frustrated, judging from the tension which was hardening his amazing features. And she wanted him inside her again. Deep and properly inside her. She wanted that more than anything.

'Would you like to come in for coffee?' she questioned carelessly.

His eyes gleamed as his tone matched hers. 'Why not?'

It was weird having the limo purr to a halt outside the purpose-built block which housed her humble bedsit and even weirder to walk into the thankfully litter-free—for once—entrance hall with Leon by her side. She wasn't used to having a man around and she certainly wasn't used to the wild flutter of her heart, or the urgent need which fired up inside her when she closed the front door and he pulled her hungrily into his arms and started kissing her as if his life depended on it.

'Leon!' she moaned and was rewarded with a taunting thrust of his hips against hers. He had pushed her jacket from her shoulders with an impatience which made her heart sing and now he was tugging frantically on the zip of her skirt, so that it pooled to a heap on the well-worn rug. Fingers flying, she did the same—easing his jacket off so that it concertinaed to the ground.

He removed her shoes and the sensible white blouse she'd worn for the court case. Next, off came her bra and panties and although both were plain and not in the least bit provocative, they still elicited a husky groan when he saw them. She could see him scanning the small room with dazed eyes before backing her towards the sofa and laying her down on it.

He hauled his silk shirt over his head without even bothering to undo all the buttons, before turning his attention to his trousers. 'Don't move,' he commanded, for he must have seen her wriggle.

But that was a big ask. Marnie could barely keep still. She wanted to writhe her bottom against the narrow sofa in joyful anticipation.

It seemed so long since that night on Para-menios, and although he had just subjected her to that blissful experience in the back of his car, she wanted something more intimate than that and didn't know how much longer she could wait.

Not much longer, it would seem as he came towards her with a look of dark intent on his face which thrilled her to the core. And it was only when he was finally and magnifi-cently naked that Marnie realised that she hadn't been able to appreciate him properly last time. The afternoon sun was far more revealing than the Greek starlight had been, accentuating the honed contours of his in-credible body so that he looked like a living statue—and much better endowed than any of those museum sculptures of her childhood.

'You're…you're beautiful,' she blurted out before she could stop herself, and the sur-prised flare of pleasure in his eyes gave *her* pleasure.

'So are you,' he husked.

She wasn't—she knew that—but by then he was bending his head to kiss each peaking nipple as if paying homage to her breasts—so that she actually *felt* beautiful. She could feel each mound fill with heat and fire, their tips so exquisitely aroused by the graze of his teeth that it felt as if she were hovering tantalisingly between pleasure and pain. He slid his hand between her legs, a moan sliding from his lips as he found her sticky warmth and began to strum against the sensitive bud until once again, Marnie found herself on the brink.

And then he was straddling her. Sliding a condom into place before entering her with one long, slick thrust. She felt him still as her body readjusted itself to his size and his width and when she looked up into his face, it was a study of concentration and fierce pleasure as he began to move.

It was incredible. It was everything Marnie had imagined it could be. It was also over very quickly. She didn't think it was possible to orgasm so rapidly, and as her body pulsed out its climax she heard the broken exclamation he made in Greek and that thrilled her too.

'Where's the bedroom?' he growled, when they finally came up for air.

She pressed her fingers into his back. 'You're in it.'

'I meant, where's the bed?'

'You're lying on it.'

'*What?*' Propping himself up on his elbow, he frowned.

'This is a studio flat,' she explained. 'Everything's in one room, including the kitchen—although the bathroom's off the hall. Haven't you ever seen a sofa bed before, Leon? If I had the energy I could demonstrate how you can tug the mattress out from underneath to make a very small double bed.'

Leon started to laugh. No, he had never seen a sofa bed before. Just as he'd never been somewhere where you shared a sleeping space with a kitchen. He yawned. 'Why don't you show me in a while and we can spend the rest of the evening here?'

She hesitated, a look of uncertainty crossing her face. 'If you're expecting dinner, I've only got leftover lasagne in the fridge.'

'I don't care what you've got in your damned fridge, Marnie. The only thing I want to feast on is you. Now stop blushing and go and get us something to drink.'

He almost regretted asking when she removed her delicious warmth from his proximity and he wished she hadn't pulled that unprepossessing white blouse over her head. Pillowing his head on his folded arms, he watched her walk across the limited space to a tiny fridge, thinking that maybe the blouse wasn't such a bad idea after all, for it ended midway down her bottom, allowing him to fully appreciate the abundant flesh of those peachy curves. She was still wearing the hold-ups—although now with a tear snaking down the back of her left leg. Should he arrange to have some silk stockings delivered? he wondered idly, before dismissing the thought. Given her spiky independence, she was more likely to garotte him with them than wear them.

She turned round, a glass of water in each hand, and as their eyes met a punch of something he didn't recognise slammed at his heart. It was desire. It must be. What else could it be? How did she do it? he wondered feverishly as he felt the inevitable hot hardening at his groin. How did she make him want her this much?

He waited until she had returned to the sofa bed and they'd drunk some water—until he had made her come with the flick of his tongue and afterwards she had licked him back as if she were slowly working her way through a large ice-cream cone. It was only then that he pushed away the pale tumble of her mussed hair.

'I think we should do this again, don't you?' he questioned idly.

He felt the sudden tension in her body.

'This?' she queried, lifting her head from his chest to stare at him, as if seeking clarification. 'Celebrating my sister's acquittal? I'm hoping she's going to avoid any more court cases, if that's what you mean.'

'You know damned well that's not what I meant, Marnie.'

'I'm a hairdresser, not a mind-reader. Could you be a bit more specific?'

Leon frowned. He would have preferred she had worked this out for herself rather than him having to spell it out. But maybe it was better this way. There would be no way she could misinterpret his bald words, nor attach any kind of unwanted significance to them.

'I'm talking about seeing one another again when I'm in town.'

'You mean for sex?' she questioned carefully.

'I suppose that's one way of describing it.' There was a pause. 'I prefer to think of it as mutual enjoyment.'

She was still regarding him with that unblinking stare. 'And you would expect me to be *available*?'

He shrugged. 'Only if you wanted to be.'

A long silence followed his remark. He realised he was hanging onto her every word and for one insane moment he actually thought she might be about to turn him down, but then those wintry eyes narrowed speculatively.

'No strings?' she said.

That was supposed to be *his* line.

'No strings,' he concurred.

'Because I'm not looking for a relationship at the moment.'

'Neither am I,' he said faintly. 'I don't want marriage and I definitely don't want children, but I—'

'You, what?' She tipped her head to one side, her blond hair falling untidily over her breasts, drawing his attention to them and making it imperative that he flick his tongue over their puckering surface as soon as possible.

'I want you,' he concluded huskily.

'Yet you're still looking shell-shocked,' she observed caustically. 'What's the matter, Leon? Haven't I been eager enough in accepting your offer? Do women usually cling to you like limpets in this kind of situation?'

'You could say that.'

'I just did.'

He smiled. 'Do you know, I don't think I've ever met a woman who answers back quite as much as you do,' he murmured as he brushed another thick and wayward strand of hair back from her face. 'But I know one guaranteed method of keeping you quiet.'

'Oh, really?' she questioned innocently. 'And what's that?'

But he shut off any further lines of questioning with a hard and demanding kiss.

CHAPTER EIGHT

THE RATHER BATTERED old Mercedes came to a halt outside the salon, the profile of the man behind the wheel darkly rugged and unmistakable, and Marnie's heart performed a predictable somersault when she saw him.

'Ooh, look—here's your boyfriend, Marnie!' Hayley, the salon junior, sounded excited as she peered out through the plate-glass windows, watching the yellow gleam of the headlights cutting through the late-September dusk. 'Haven't seen him in a while.'

'No. That's right. He's been away,' said Marnie, grabbing her coat and feasting her eyes on her Greek lover, who was waiting for her in his old car. The ten-year-old car he kept in his garage for solo anonymous driving trips until she'd confessed she much preferred it to his sleek, chauffeur-driven limo. Just as she'd explained she'd rather get the bus than be driven around by someone wearing a cap and uniform who insisted on leaping to open the door for her as if she were infirm, and bowing to her every wish. At first Leon had thought she was joking—as if nobody in their right mind wouldn't like being ferried around by a driver. But Marnie hadn't been joking. What was happening to her was surreal enough anyway—without throwing into the mix the sort of hands-on luxury most people only dreamed about. His massive apartment she could just about cope with, along with the staff he employed there—but anything else would be stretching it. And why get used to something which was only ever intended to be temporary? Wouldn't that make the inevitable comedown even worse?

Wasn't she already terrified of how much she was going to miss him once it ended?

'Where's he been?'

Marnie turned to look at the salon junior. 'Oh, you know. Abroad. On business.'

Hayley frowned. 'You've never really said what it is he does, Marnie.'

'Something to do with property?' Marnie said, turning the answer into a question. 'I'm never really sure what it is myself.'

Slinging her handbag over her shoulder, she

grimaced. She hadn't actually *lied* to the staff at Hair Heaven about the identity of her 'boyfriend', and particularly not to young Hayley, whom she'd been mentoring for years—she'd just played down Leon's international status and achievements. Because the reasons for her caginess had the same root as her preference for travelling in a nondescript rather than a head-turning car. It was easier to let her colleagues believe she was going out with an ordinary man, rather than an international property tycoon, and it stopped them from asking too many questions.

She licked her lips. Not that 'going out' was a particularly accurate description of their set-up. They didn't really travel anywhere much beyond the walls of his vast apartment—although, to be fair, he often asked if she wanted to go out for dinner, or the theatre, or even the opera. But Marnie invariably refused and not just because she was paranoid about their relationship going public. She liked being alone with him best of all, without the pressure of wondering whether she was using the correct knife and fork. And besides, she didn't have the clothes to wear to those places and she didn't want people staring at them, thinking what an odd couple they made. She could never quite shrug off the feeling that others were judging her and deciding she didn't have a right to be there. She knew that was called imposter syndrome.

Because you are an imposter. If Leon knew the person you really were, you wouldn't get within five yards of his home.

Because that was the bottom line, wasn't it? The ever-present fear which always gnawed away at the back of her mind, that her true identity would be rumbled. And not just that. Years of being rejected and subjected to the harsh regimes within the many institutions which had housed her had planted in her the seeds of doubt. Of not being good enough—certainly not good enough for a man of Leon's calibre. Cocooned in the roomy opulence of his London home, she was safe from speculation, and safety was something she had always rated highly.

Only Pansy knew the truth about Marnie's new lover and Pansy most definitely did not approve. She seemed to have become a worrier on her sister's behalf and, in a slightly ironic twist, their lifelong roles seemed to have become reversed.

'Is that why he bailed me out?' her twin had demanded. 'Just so he could get inside your knickers? You do know that he has a terrible reputation with women, don't you, Marnie? I looked him up on the internet. Why, even *I* wouldn't dream of getting involved with a man like that, and I'm way more experienced than you!'

That last bit had been particularly wounding and Marnie had railed at her sister's ungratefulness, closing her mind to the fears which Pansy's words had produced. If her twin was determined to be cynical, that was up to her. She had agreed to a no-strings fling with Leon. She had laid down those terms herself and the billionaire tycoon had agreed to them. She'd done that mostly to protect herself, to try to shield herself against any hurt she might feel when it all ended—and if she was being naïve, then so what? Naivety wasn't a crime, was it? He had given her the opportunity to walk away from him and she had chosen not to take it.

Hayley's question broke into her thoughts. 'He's still keen, then, I take it?'

Marnie gave a ghost of a smile as she made her way towards the door. 'That's a question you'd have to ask him, I guess.'

But one word spun around in her head as

she bade goodnight to the junior and pushed open the salon door.

Keen?

He was keen for sex, that was for sure. Just like she was. And that was what all this was about, she reminded herself fiercely. A grown-up relationship which revolved around the physical, with no unrealistic promises and definitely no glimpses into a possible future. They never discussed next month, let alone next year. He hadn't asked how she was spending Christmas or quizzed her about what she wanted for her birthday. In fact, he had no idea when her birthday was, and she didn't know his either. And since Marnie had never pursued a happy-ever-after, she had convinced herself that she was contented with what Leon was offering.

Sometimes she couldn't quite believe the situation in which she found herself, because in a sense she was betraying everything she held dear. Sometimes, in the dead of night, she found herself unable to escape the mocking thoughts which taunted her. That she had become something she'd never set out to be. A rich man's plaything. Something she'd never planned but which had been driven by her fierce desire for him. Because she just couldn't resist him. Never. He only had to look at her to make her boneless with longing, and when he touched her she went up in flames.

She'd let down the defences she'd spent a lifetime erecting and knew that made her vulnerable. But Marnie had convinced herself that as long as she compartmentalised everything—if she kept her feelings in check and just enjoyed the sex—she would be able to keep emotional danger at bay.

Hayley was still standing at the salon window watching as Marnie opened the car door and there was Leon in the driver's seat, his jaw shadowed, his black hair ruffled. She felt her pulse pick up speed as he turned to slant her that slow and sexy smile.

'Hi,' he said softly.

'Hi.'

Keeping her greeting as casual as his, Marnie slid into the passenger seat and snapped her seat belt shut. How quickly she had adapted to being a rich man's lover! His discreet squeeze of her thigh made her shiver and a rush of something powerful flooded through her as their gazes met. But there was no kiss. Nothing to indicate he'd been missing her while he'd been away. Leon Kanonidou didn't do public declarations of affection. Just as he didn't do romance, or commitment, or marriage—though he'd never told her why and she'd never asked. They didn't have that kind of soul-searching relationship.

But that was okay.

That was what she had signed up for, wasn't it?

'Like to go for a drive?' he questioned as he started up the engine. 'We could watch the sun go down somewhere along the river. Maybe have a drink on the way.'

The dying September day might be growing dusky, but it was still light enough for Marnie to notice the tension which was forming deep grooves on either side of his lips. Was that jet lag? she wondered. 'We don't have to. You look tired—and I've been on my feet all day,' she said, suddenly realising how much the backs of her calves were aching. 'Why don't we go...' she nearly said home, until she realised that sounded a little presumptuous, so she quickly changed course '...back to yours?'

'Okay. Back to mine it is.' Leon switched on the ignition and glanced in his rear-view mirror as he pulled away. 'Why don't you tell me about your day?'

Out of the corner of his eye Leon could see her clasping her hands together on her lap, before beginning to chat. Slowly at first and then, as she got more into her stride, her account became rapidly laced with irreverent anecdotes and a few impersonations of the salon's clientele, which for once failed to make him smile.

His mouth hardened as he drove into the underground garage of his block. Deep down, he was grateful she had refused his offer of a drive because he was worn out after his trip and dreading the week ahead. He switched off the engine. Sex would ease some of the tension. It always did.

The elevator from the garage took them straight to his apartment and as Marnie removed her rather ugly coat he felt the instant flare of hunger. He stared at her with a bemusement which was rapidly overtaken by desire, despite her sartorial shortcomings. Beneath the coat she wore a plain and frumpy blouse and skirt, along with a pair of shoes whose only possible attribute—surely—was that they could be described as *comfortable*. But at least she had untied her hair, letting it fall into a silken tumble which rippled down over her luscious breasts, in the style she knew he liked. She was the sexiest woman he'd ever met and yet she dressed like a middle-aged secretary.

He shook his head a little, still slightly irritated by her stubborn rebuttal of his suggested gifts, despite the fact that they'd been seeing each other for weeks now. She hadn't let him buy her anything. No clothes. No jewels. No shoes. Nothing. Not a single trinket had ever made its way from him to her and he found that deeply frustrating. No woman had ever refused his gifts before and sometimes he found himself wondering if she thought he would regard her more favourably if she rejected his generosity.

But at other times he chided himself for his cynicism because—quite simply—she took his breath away. He let his gaze drift over her now, unable to lose his faint air of incredulity. Wondering how it was that, despite her modest wardrobe and lack of sophistication, Marnie Porter could provoke in him the most powerful physical response he'd ever experienced. A response which was all-consuming, instant and automatic. She was doing it now, without doing *anything*—just regarding him with those watchful grey eyes which gave nothing away.

He had tried to analyse her appeal, with varying degrees of success. Sometimes he thought it was because she made him laugh and challenged him all at the same time. At others, because she seemed genuinely unimpressed by his wealth. Was it because she didn't bore him with questions about how he *felt*—or, even worse, give him chapter on verse on her own feelings? Or was it more primitive than that? Maybe it was all tied up with him having been her only lover. Maybe he was more old-fashioned than he'd thought.

Exclusivity was a powerful entity, he concluded wryly, his lips softening in anticipation. And purity was a surprisingly potent concept. He could feel a sweet aching in his balls as hot, hard desire flooded through him. A desire strong enough to take his mind off the forthcoming engagement which was looming ever closer in his diary with all the allure of an execution.

Deliberately, he leaned back against the wall. 'Come here,' he instructed softly, his concerns drifting away as she went straight into his waiting arms. Wasn't it remarkable that she knew intuitively when to be docile and when to be dominant and, right now, he was the one who needed to be in total control. He kissed her for a while. A long while. Until her breath had begun to quicken. Until he was so hard that he wanted to explode. But he liked making himself hold back—and that was part of the control too.

'How…how was your trip?' she asked breathlessly, as he slid her blouse from her shoulders.

'Predictable.'

'Oh?'

As her skirt pooled to the ground, he put his hand between her thighs and felt her shiver as his thumb alighted on her sensitive nub, already slick with desire. 'Well, we *could* talk about my trip,' he said unevenly, flipping her round so that now it was *her* back pressed against the wall. 'Or we could talk about how wet you are and how much I want to be inside you again, after a wait which has felt almost unendurable.' He swallowed. 'The choice is yours, Marnie.'

'That's not…fair,' she said weakly as he pushed aside the damp gusset of her panties and grazed his fingertip down over her soft folds.

'Isn't it? How would you like me to be fair, then, *agape mou*?' he mocked, his movement pausing. 'Do you want me to stop? To fix you a drink, and remark how beautiful the trees look from the terrace?'

'No,' she husked. 'You know I don't.'

He gave a soft laugh as he unzipped himself and let his trousers fall, before stroking on a condom and hooking up her legs, so that her thighs clamped themselves deliciously around his hips.

He could have come immediately but tempered his own desire until she was engulfed by satisfaction, until her curvy body tensed with waves of release and she shuddered out his name. With one final jerk he let go and spilled his seed—pumping ecstatically until at last he stilled inside her spasming flesh.

Afterwards, he kicked off his jeans and carried her into the bedroom, laying her down in the centre of his bed so that her hair was spread like rippling gold against the pristine white of the pillow, thinking how exquisite she looked with her eyelids hooded and that dreamy smile curving her lips. Deftly, he removed the rest of their clothes and pulled her into his arms, so that her soft flesh moulded against his beneath the duvet.

'I really am the most inattentive of hosts.' He pressed his lips into her hair. 'Want me to get you a drink now?'

'No, thanks. And for what it's worth—I have no complaints about your hosting skills,' she said, rolling over onto her stomach and fixing him with that curious grey gaze. 'I'm more interested in how you are. You look stressed.'

'Not any more, I hope.' He yawned. 'Orgasm is supposed to release stress.'

'Temporarily, I believe. But now it's back again. I can tell.'

'You're very observant.' He yawned again.

'Mmm. I know. It's an acquired skill. Comes from years of watching people in the mirror. I can always tell if there's something on their mind. And there's definitely something on yours.' She hesitated for a moment before she started speaking very carefully, as if she were reading from a crib sheet. 'Do you want to…to move on?'

'Move on?' He looked at her with genuine bewilderment. 'Move on where?'

'From me.'

His eyes narrowed as it slowly dawned on him what she meant. It was honest and up-front but if she was expecting him to make a declaration that he would never leave her, then she was about to be disappointed. 'No, Marnie. I don't want that but when I do, I can assure you that you'll be the first to know. Is that a deal?' He wondered if she would find his honesty unsettling, but her careless shrug reassured him.

'Deal,' she said, turning onto her side to face him. 'So, now do you want to tell me what's bothering you?'

'You don't usually ask questions.'

'No, but you don't usually keep scowling like that either.'

Leon stared into the up-close focus of her features because the crazy thing was that he *did* want to tell her. Crazy because his usual instinct would be to shut the topic right down. But there was something about the way she was talking which felt more like concern than prying. He didn't get the feeling she wanted to discover more about him because that would increase her influence over him, or because one day she might try to use it against him. He was no stranger to power games with women, but there had never been any with her. In fact, she had been the soul of discretion since their affair had begun. She'd explained that she hadn't told anyone at work about it—'They'd only try to talk me out of it, like my sister.'—which he had found slightly insulting. Her words had been backed up by a lack of prurient calls from diary columnists, trying to find out why he was dating someone like her.

He swallowed. She was unlike any woman he'd ever known, that was for sure. She confounded his expectations at every turn. Was that why he was tempted to confide in her? Because, on some unfamiliar level, he felt he could trust her not to take this any further?

'My father is getting married and I have to go to the wedding.'

'Have to?' Her grey eyes narrowed. 'I can't imagine you doing anything you don't want to, Leon.'

'Your faith is touching.' His voice hardened. 'Put it this way—the publicity and conjecture surrounding a no-show would be far worse.'

She pushed a thick handful of hair away from her flushed face. 'Let me guess. You don't like your new stepmother?'

The suggestion was almost comic in the circumstances but Leon didn't smile. 'It would be difficult to attribute that particular role to a woman who, at twenty-four, is almost a decade my junior.'

'So she's—'

'I think the term you might be looking for

is trophy wife,' he offered caustically. 'And there's no need to look so concerned, Marnie—I'm used to it. This will be my father's fourth wedding, but the third was far worse—or rather, that particular stepmother was.'

There was a pause. Her soft lips became suddenly sombre, as if she had detected the new and bitter note which had entered his voice.

'So was she *cruel*, like in all the fairy tales?'

The silence which followed was broken only by the sound of their breathing. 'No,' he said, at last. 'I almost wish she had been.' He waited for her to comment because that would have been a distraction—an intrusion—and might have halted the dark flow of his words. But when she didn't, he found himself lost in the past. Talking as if nobody were listening. Saying things to Marnie Porter that he'd never told another soul.

CHAPTER NINE

'MY FATHER WAS a shipbuilder,' Leon began, pushing the sheet away from his bare torso. 'And one of the wealthiest men in Greece.'

His words faded away and for a moment Marnie thought he'd forgotten she was there. 'That explains how you got so rich, I guess,' she prompted.

'Actually, it doesn't.' His words became coated with acid. 'I took nothing from him.'

'Isn't that unusual?' she questioned slowly. 'For a man not to help his kids out financially?'

'I believe so. Though he certainly didn't have any problem showering wealth on my two older stepbrothers from his first marriage. But by the time I was a teenager, we were estranged.'

There was a space in the conversation which demanded to be filled. 'Why was that?'

He shrugged. 'It's a long story.'

'Most stories are.'

He was staring at her, but it was as though he were looking right through her, and suddenly Marnie found herself wishing they were making love again or that she'd let him fix her that drink after all. Something which might have distracted him long enough to change his mind about telling her this. Because wasn't that the trouble when you found out more about someone—that you might not necessarily like what you heard? That once you had started exchanging confidences it changed the nature of a relationship and meant you might never be able to return to an earlier, easier place? Wasn't there the fear that he might expect her to tell him stuff about herself?

And she could never risk that happening.

She swallowed down the lump in her throat, knowing it would be better to halt the conversation right now. Make an excuse to leave their sex-rumpled bed to get them a drink or something and hope that he'd forgotten about it by the time she returned.

But it was too late for any U-turn. She could feel the rough brush of his thigh against hers as he changed position on the bed and turned to face her, his handsome features hard as granite, with an expression she'd never seen there before. 'My mother died when I was sixteen,' he began.

'I'm sorry,' she said, but she spoke with almost exaggerated care, because life with mothers was not her favourite topic. 'What happened?'

'She had cancer for a long time.' He paused. 'A fact made worse by the fact she didn't tell me how bad it was. She pretended there was nothing wrong right up until the end and by the time I found out…'

She saw and heard the pain as his words faded out and wished she could take it away. 'I think terminal illness was handled very differently when we were growing up,' she said, with some degree of calm. 'They tried to protect children from the truth without recognising the damage they were doing in the process. Didn't your father say anything to you, or did he collude with her?'

He shook his head. 'It wasn't a case of collusion. They barely spoke. He was never around and I don't think he particularly cared what happened to her,' he said, and now she could hear a different kind of bitterness in his voice. 'It was his second marriage and not a particularly happy one, but at that stage in his life I don't think he had the appetite for another divorce. So he just carried on seeing his long-term mistress and once my mother had died, he married her.'

She took a moment to absorb this. 'So what was that like? For you?'

He turned away from her, lying on his back to stare up at the ceiling—but not before Marnie had seen the flicker of something unbearably bleak in his eyes. It was only afterwards that she realised it was disgust.

'It was hell,' he said bitterly. 'She…'

'She what?' she prompted softly.

'My stepmother was a very beautiful woman and very conscious of that fact, in the way that beautiful women sometimes are,' he said. 'My father was in his fifties when I was born, so by the time he remarried, he was relatively old.'

'While you were just on the brink of manhood,' she observed. 'I'm guessing the atmosphere in the house wasn't great.'

'It was toxic. There were warped undercurrents everywhere you moved and you wouldn't need to be a genius to work out what happened.' He turned back towards her. 'Or rather, what my stepmother intended to happen.'

She didn't like what she could see in his eyes now, but she could hardly deny the truth when it was staring her in the face. 'She...' Marnie's stomach gave a sickening lurch. 'She wanted you?'

He nodded. 'Oh, she wanted me, all right. It was a silent form of seduction, conducted in total secrecy. Lingering glances which used to make my flesh crawl. She used to slide her tongue over her lips whenever she stared at me and she stared at me a *lot*. Nobody but me would have known it was happening, but I knew. It's what made me despise women who use and abuse their sexuality.' His words were tight and clipped. 'I kept away from the house as much as I could, but soon my absences started to be noticed. My father wanted to know why I was never there.'

'And you couldn't tell him, I suppose.'

'Of course I couldn't tell him. It would have ruined him. Smashed his pride and his ego, and no way did I hate him enough to want to do that.' He gave a contemptuous laugh. 'I don't think he would have believed me anyway—for what man likes to believe he's being cuckolded? The upshot was that I felt like a stranger in my own house. As if I were trespassing within the hallowed sanctuary of their marital home—and my father rein-forced that feeling in his attitude towards me. Maybe I reminded him too much of the wife he had cheated on, or maybe on some sublim-inal level he *did* guess what my stepmother's intentions were.' A muscle began to work at his temple. 'All I know is that he was totally in thrall to that woman in a way I've never forgotten, nor wanted to replicate.'

His words unsettled her—sent alarm bells ringing—but Marnie told herself this wasn't about her, or her insipient fears about *their* re-lationship. 'Don't they call it the young lion syndrome?' she questioned slowly. 'Who is driven out of the pack by the older, jealous male.'

'I guess.'

She took the opportunity to snuggle up to him. 'So what did you do?'

'I took the route of disenchanted sons the world over and ran away to America. To Chi-cago, which has a big Greek community. I found myself a job and a mentor who told me what I needed to do. And with his backing, eventually I got lucky.'

'That sounds a very modest assessment, Leon,' she said, drawing a circle over his belly with the tip of her finger.

'Are you implying that I'm usually immodest?' he mocked, shifting his weight slightly to give her better access.

'I wouldn't dream of it!' Her face grew serious. 'But now you're reconciled with him? You must be, if you're going to his wedding.'

He shrugged. 'In theory—though it was never a total severing of relations, for that would have caused gossip and I had no desire to bring shame upon the family name. Whenever I visited my homeland I made sure I saw him, though I never visited the family house because I didn't want to run into my stepmother. But there was a definite thawing when he finally divorced her on grounds of infidelity.' He let out a frustrated sigh. 'And then came the news that he was planning to marry a woman in her twenties. Nearly sixty years his junior this time round.'

'And he wants you there.'

'He wants me there.'

'But you don't want to go?'

His mouth twisted. 'What do you think?'

'I'm thinking that maybe your conscience is nudging you to,' she answered quietly. 'Because he's an old man and it probably means a lot to him.'

Leon tensed, aware that again she had surprised him with her perception and quiet lack of judgement. She had listened to his words but his confidences hadn't brought forth a torrent of prurient questions. It was as though he'd dropped a stone into a pool, leaving behind no ripples. As if the things he had told her had vanished without trace.

And suddenly it occurred to him that perhaps Marnie Porter would be the ideal person to take to the wedding as his plus-one. Wouldn't she be like a breath of fresh air in that stale and echoing mansion? Someone innocent and straightforward who wasn't motivated by avarice, or greed. Someone honest and truthful, who could provide him with enough entertainment and satisfaction to make the whole damned occasion bearable.

He reached up to twirl a strand of pale hair around his finger and when he let it go it dangled in a perfect spiral against her heart-shaped face. 'Want to come with me?' he asked.

She blinked. 'Where?'

'To Syros, for my father's wedding.'

'You mean to the marriage of a child bride to a man you have a rocky relationship with? You haven't exactly sold it to me, Leon,' she said, but the waver in her voice betrayed a sudden sense of nervousness. 'I'm guessing it'll be a big, glittering affair?'

'Not at all. My father assures me it will be very low-key. A handful of guests, that's all.'

She still didn't look convinced. 'When is it?'

'Next weekend. The wedding is on Sunday,' he said. 'We could fly out on Thursday and come back on Monday. Make a break of it. We don't have to stay on Syros. I've recently bought a property in Thessaloniki. I think you'd like it.'

'I'm sure I would, but I happen to be working on Saturday.'

His eyes narrowed thoughtfully. Most women would have walked over broken glass to get an invitation to a party at the famous Kanonidou mansion and Marnie's reluctance was only firing his determination to have her there. Idly, he reached for her breast and began to caress the pliant flesh. 'But surely—'

'Surely what, Leon?' Pushing his hand away, she sat up and glared at him. 'You think I can just drop everything and come with you when you snap your fingers? You obviously have no idea how a hairdressing salon works! I have a client list which I've built up over years and which I'm not going to jeopardise for some random last-minute invitation.'

'"Some random last-minute invitation…"' he repeated faintly as he pulled her back down and into his arms, and this time she didn't resist.

'Well, how else would you describe it? You've hardly given me weeks to prepare, have you?' Undoubtedly influenced by the fingers which were edging towards her inner thigh, her voice became smoky. 'If I were to agree to come—*if*—it would have to be when I've finished work on Saturday afternoon.'

'That won't be a problem. We can fly out that night. You've never been on my plane, have you?'

'No, I've never been on your plane, but I haven't been losing any sleep over it.'

'That's a surprise. Most women are turned on by the size of a man's jet,' he said softly as he pinned his thigh over hers.

'Oh, you're impossible!'

'Am I?'

'Totally.'

He grazed his mouth over hers. 'But you're going to have to let me buy you some clothes for the wedding.'

Her eyes snapped open. 'No.'

'Yes,' he insisted softly.

'You know how I feel about you buying me things.'

'I don't think I could ever be in any doubt about that, Marnie,' he said drily. 'But this is different.'

'Because I dress so terribly, you mean?'

He chose his words with care. 'Because otherwise, I think you might feel out of place. And that would draw attention to you, which I know you don't like.'

She went very quiet then, as if she were weighing up her options. 'I'm not going into one of those fancy stores where the assistants look you up and down as if you're a nasty smell,' she said eventually.

A smile touched his lips, because this felt something close to triumph. 'That isn't going to happen. You don't have to do anything you don't want to, Marnie.'

CHAPTER TEN

THE PILE OF glossy merchandise was piled high on the floor of Leon's dressing room and Marnie came to a sudden halt when she saw it. Taking off her coat, she draped it over the back of a chair, conscious of his bright blue gaze boring into her. 'What's all this?' she asked slowly.

'Why don't you take a look?'

She regarded the boxes and upmarket carrier bags as warily as if they contained a set of unexploded bombs, but really it had been a disingenuous question. She knew exactly what would be inside—outfits for her to wear to his father's wedding, which she had grudgingly agreed to accept. She'd told herself that such a move made sense because if she turned up looking like a poor relation, wouldn't that make her stand out even more? But now the moment had arrived, her heart was thumping and she couldn't seem to shake off a gnawing feeling of anxiety. Was that because accepting his gifts seemed to signify a subtle shift of power between them? Or was she being delusional in denying that Leon had *always* possessed the power in their relationship? She wasn't sure—all she did know was that she felt as if she had crossed a line and the boundaries between them were becoming blurred.

Leon had suggested she choose the clothes herself but she had refused—citing busyness at work making it impossible for her to find the time. But the truth—which she didn't tell him—was that she wouldn't have known where to start looking. What if she'd broken some fundamental style rule and turned up wearing something horribly unsuitable? More than that, she couldn't bear the thought of walking into an intimidating store brandishing a rich man's credit card because that would have made her feel like…like a cliché.

She bit her lip.

Like a kept woman.

Perhaps if she'd been able to get hold of her sister she might have asked her to accompany her, because Pansy was super-confident, even if their taste in clothes clashed. But her twin wasn't answering her phone and, besides, Marnie couldn't bear to endure another lecture on Leon's unsuitability as a lover.

The upshot was that Leon had announced he would sort it out himself—and it appeared he had done just that. Was there anything a rich man couldn't do? she marvelled silently.

She walked across the room towards the goodies, telling herself she didn't particularly *care* what he'd bought her, but that certainty was fading by the second and suddenly Marnie was back to being that little girl at Christmas time. The one who never got any decent presents, even though she'd never stopped hoping. Even when she and Pansy were being considered for adoption, the gifts they received were always second-rate. It was as if their prospective parents didn't want to waste any money in case it didn't work out, which, of course, it never did—which meant that her mistrust of generosity ran deep. But Leon was looking at her questioningly as she stood in front of all the designer-store bounty—and surely it would be rude not to take a peek…

Crouching down, she began to untie the silken ribbons, delving between rustling layers of tissue paper to pull out the kind of clothes she'd only ever seen her most upmarket clients wearing. Several filmy day dresses, a couple of delicate blouses and butter-soft T-shirts. Pale jeans and a beautifully-cut skirt, as well as a kaftan, sandals and swimwear—all with co-ordinating accessories. There was underwear, too. Flimsy little scraps of fine lace and satin. High-cut panties designed to flatter a woman's legs and bras whose sole purpose, she suspected, would be to accentuate cleavage. Yet instinctively she knew that all these colours were *her* colours and that everything would flatter her and fit her perfectly. They were exactly the kind of clothes she might have chosen if she had lived a different life and been a different person.

But it was the dress which had obviously been chosen for the ceremony itself which commanded centre stage. In the softest scarlet silk imaginable, it was the loveliest thing she had ever seen. Marnie swallowed as she ran her fingertips over the slippery fabric, slightly scared by just how much she longed to wear it, but her natural suspicion was never far from the surface.

'Where did all these things come from?' she questioned, forcing herself to let the garment slide from her fingers. 'Did the good fairy drop them by?'

'The stylist delivered them this afternoon.'

'A stylist who's never met me?' She raised her eyebrows. 'She must be very perceptive.'

'Actually, the stylist was a he.'

'Oh. Right. And how did *he* know my size?'

'I gave him your measurements.'

'I wasn't aware you *knew* my measurements, Leon!'

He gave a slow smile. 'Let's just say I have a good eye for dimensions.'

The ugly twist of jealousy inside her made Marnie unable to hold back her feelings, even though caution advised her against expressing them. 'I suppose you've kitted out countless women like this in the past?'

'No, I haven't,' he negated silkily. 'And I've certainly never gone to the trouble of finding the best stylist in the business and telling him exactly what I thought you needed.'

Her voice was cautious. 'And what was that?'

His gaze swept over her. 'Beautiful things which weren't too revealing, because you have an essential modesty about you, Marnie, and I like that. In fact, I like it a lot. Call me old-fashioned but the possession of virtue is a dying art and it's seriously underrated.' His voice deepened. 'Though I can't understand why you insist on covering up so much, when you have the most beautiful body I've ever seen.'

It was a rare compliment, which made her heart stab with joy and apprehension, and Marnie busied herself with scouring through another bag, hoping the movement would hide the sudden hotness in her cheeks. He was making her sound like the personification of all that was good and innocent, but the woman he was talking about was nothing but a fiction. Yes, she had been a virgin, but he was making her sound like some kind of saint and she definitely did not have a saint's pedigree.

Worry began to gnaw away at the pit of her stomach as she wondered just where this affair of theirs was going.

Ever since he'd asked her to accompany him to the wedding, she had been aware of straying into perilous waters. With each day that passed, she felt the growing danger of remaining in this relationship. It was as though she were sleepwalking her way towards the inevitable pain of rejection, by a man whose company was never intended to be anything other than temporary.

And all the warning signs were staring her

in the face—signs she had been stubbornly refusing to heed. Leon had told her about his surprisingly painful past. His mother's failure to disclose her terminal illness must have seemed like a terrible betrayal. He had witnessed other betrayals, too. His father's infidelity and slavish devotion to a new wife, who had tried to seduce his son.

No wonder he was so set against marriage and permanence.

And if he was? So what? What on earth did that have to do with her?

Her flush deepened.

Unless she was seriously considering herself in the role of Leon Kanonidou's wife! What had happened to the stubborn sense of determination with which she had entered into this affair? Hadn't her number one criterion for agreeing to become his de facto mistress been that it could only succeed if she kept the physical and the emotional separate? It was supposed to be about sex. Nothing else.

Nothing else.

'Well?'

She looked up to see Leon staring at her, his expression indicating he was awaiting her verdict, and she realised how ungrateful she must seem. He'd obviously gone to a lot of trouble to buy these gorgeous clothes, yet she was acting as if he'd committed a crime. And she had agreed to this, hadn't she? She had agreed to let him dress her up like a doll. Rising to her feet, she walked towards him, wrapping her arms around his neck and kissing him on the lips. 'I love them—every one of them,' she said truthfully.

'So why don't you try on the red dress?' he suggested.

She took a step back. 'What, now?'

'Don't you want to see what it looks like on?' His voice deepened. 'I know I do.'

It was a tacit request to take off her dowdy work clothes and replace them with a fairy-tale dress and, although Marnie tried to convince herself that would be a lovely thing to do, she suddenly felt stricken with shyness. Leon had watched her undress countless times before, so why did this feel so *different*?

Beneath the burn of his gaze she self-consciously removed her jumper and skirt and laid them on the chair to join her coat. She felt like one of those snakes she'd once seen on a TV documentary. As if she were shedding her old skin and taking on a brand-new persona—someone she didn't know or recognise.

She was down to just her underwear when

Leon began to walk towards her and she knew from his expression—which was hard and hot and hungry—just what he wanted. What *she* wanted, too—because wouldn't sex successfully eradicate the muddle of her thoughts?

'On second thought,' he said, 'the dress can wait.'

And the crazy thing was that Marnie didn't make a single objection to his masterful assertion. As he pulled her into his arms she shivered with anticipation, her stomach dissolving, her blood growing heated with need. Because that was the fundamental weakness which flew in the face of her certainty that she was getting in too deep—that the moment Leon touched her, she couldn't think straight.

His kiss was urgent and she moaned beneath the seeking pressure of his lips. As he slid her panties down over her trembling thighs something told her she would never wear this old underwear again. That from now on she would be dressed in fine satin and silk and lace, like a pampered woman.

Like a mistress.

She felt him tugging urgently at his belt as vulnerability and desire washed over her. 'I haven't had a shower yet. I still smell of the salon,' she whispered.

'I like the smell of the salon, but all I can smell is you,' he growled, kicking off the remainder of his clothes and carrying her next door into the bedroom, where he laid her down on the huge bed, and straddled her.

He took his time. He stroked her, knowing exactly how she liked to be touched—but something told her he was teasing her, too. By now she badly wanted him inside her but still he held back. As if he were hell-bent on demonstrating his steely self-control—or her lack of it—as she begged him to take her. As if it gave him a heady kick of power when he elicited her first helpless orgasm with the quick dart of his tongue. 'Oh!' she cried. 'Oh!'

He entered her when she was still caught up in those powerful spasms and as he filled her a soft warmth flooded through her body. She must have gasped something appreciative because his gaze was now focussed on her intently. And when he looked at her that way at a time like this she felt closer to him than she'd ever felt to anyone. 'Leon,' she breathed, overcome with an unwanted emotion which threatened to rock the foundations of her world.

'What is it, Marnie?' he mocked.

Closing her eyes, she bit back the tender

words which were threatening to spill from her lips and concentrated on the ripples of pleasure instead. Already so close to the edge, she buried her head in his neck and began to husk out another orgasm, her fingernails digging into his broad shoulders as he followed her, choking out that incomprehensible sound he always made when he was coming and which had become so familiar to her. They lay there for a while in silence, his fingers running through her hair, when his question came right out of the blue.

'So what happened to make you so modest and shy, Marnie Porter?'

She fought her instinct to freeze, in case she looked as though she had something to hide.

Because you have.

'I don't know if that's a very accurate description.' She forced herself to smile. 'People always say I'm very mouthy.'

'Well, you are. Sometimes.' He smoothed a lock of hair away from her cheek. 'But you are also very reserved. And I'm curious why.'

She wanted to jump up from the bed and run away. She wanted to tell him it was none of his business and if this was only supposed to be a casual relationship, then he had no right to ask her questions. But he had told her all that stuff about himself and if she kept quiet that would only make him suspicious. Men like him didn't like having things denied them. He would probably start probing and she would have to stonewall him and then they'd have a terrible row.

And she didn't want it to end like this.

She chewed on the inside of her mouth. She could explain some things. Just not all of them. That was a compromise of sorts, wasn't it? 'You haven't actually met my sister, have you?'

'No, but I've seen a photo of her.'

'Then you will have seen for yourself how beautiful she is.'

'She's certainly a dramatic dresser.' He shrugged. 'If you must know, I don't think she's nearly as beautiful as you.'

'Oh, come *on*, Leon,' she said crossly, edging away a fraction. 'You don't have to flatter me because we've just had sex! We're non-identical twins and, yes, we're very similar, but beauty is notoriously difficult to define. A centimetre here and a centimetre there makes all the difference and it's Pansy who has the biggest eyes and the better figure and she was the one who…'

'The one who, what?' he questioned softly as her voice tailed away.

'It doesn't matter.'

'Or maybe it does.'

His voice was compelling. It was binding her to him like the strong silk of a spider's web. It enveloped her and in that present moment it made her feel safe and protected. Was it that which made her speak almost without thinking? 'I told you how we spent a lot of our time in the care system—'

'Sure. Because your mother—'

'Died,' she said quickly and now she was *keen* to talk to him, because surely one frank disclosure would rule out the need for another. 'We had no other relatives. And back then—it may have changed now—the care system used to employ some pretty dodgy people. The sort of people who might take an unhealthy interest in a pretty little blonde girl. I was always looking out for Pansy and I tried...'

'You tried to shield her,' he said, his voice tight with repressed fury. 'Let me guess. You did everything you could to help conceal her burgeoning sexuality from those bastards.'

Marnie stared at him. 'How can you even *know* that?'

'It's pretty obvious. I'm also guessing you taught yourself to hide behind concealing clothes and made Pansy do the same—and the moment she was able to take care of herself, she probably rebelled against that. You, on the other hand, kept up the habit.' He frowned. 'One thing which has always puzzled me is why you were wearing that uncharacteristically flimsy orange bikini when we met.'

'Oh, that. My work colleagues in London gave it to me before I flew out to Greece, mainly as a joke.' She turned her face towards his. 'If it hadn't been for that—if I'd been wearing one of my all-concealing swimsuits—do you think you'd still have taken me out on your motorbike and then to dinner?'

'Truthfully?' He shrugged. 'I have no idea. I certainly wasn't impervious to the very obvious visual stimulus of your barely clothed body, but there was also a powerful spark between us which went beyond the merely physical, Marnie.' There was a pause. 'There still is,' he concluded silkily.

Marnie pursed her lips together, trying to keep her reaction hidden. She wanted to thank him for saying that, which probably said a lot about her lack of self-esteem. But the trouble was that his murmured words gave her hope—and false hope could have painful consequences. Sexual chemistry was nothing special. It was fleeting and transient. Everyone knew that—and woe betide the person who thought otherwise.

'I'm going for a shower,' she said, sliding out of bed before he could try to change her mind, and it wasn't until she was standing beneath the steaming jets that she realised she was shaking.

She closed her eyes as hot water rained down on her face. Leon had asked all the right questions—or maybe they were the wrong questions—because she had ended up revealing more about herself than she ever did. More than she was comfortable with. And confidences were like standing at the top of a slippery slope. Once she'd told him one thing, he would want to hear more. And still more. Her sleazy beginnings were fascinating to other people—she remembered that much from school, when someone had found out about their mother. She remembered the row which had resulted after she and Pansy had been taunted and how the school had asked for them to be removed, because they really couldn't have little girls fighting like that.

And yet another set of foster parents had explained to the authorities that they wouldn't be adopting the twin girls, with the faces of angels.

There was a *reason* why she had always felt as if she were on the outside, looking in—and why she would always stay that way. Because she was. People like her were scarred by their experiences and sometimes those scars were too deep to ever heal properly. She had never felt 'normal' and probably never would. She had always accepted that, until she had met Leon. He had made her want to step out of her comfort zone. He had made her want things which had never even been on her radar before and that was so dangerous.

She went back into the bedroom to get dressed, relieved he was nowhere to be seen, and as she pulled on some of her new lingerie she knew she couldn't carry on like this, no matter how much she liked Leon Kanonidou.

Liked?

She almost laughed out loud. Who was she trying to kid?

'Liked' was a lacklustre description of her feelings for him. Lately Leon had been dominating her thoughts like an addiction, and whenever she saw him it was as if an invisible fist had reached inside her chest and squeezed her heart very hard. She'd never felt love before but that didn't mean she was immune to it or its power. Did it? And if that was the case it was only going to get worse. If she allowed her feelings free rein they could easily overwhelm her, and then who would she be? Just another foolish woman sobbing into her pillow because she'd fallen into the trap of thinking a man might change.

Leon had told her from the start what he didn't want and she had gone along with that. And surely if he got any inkling that she'd started to want more, he would move to end it anyway.

She sucked in a deep breath.

She would go to the wedding, as planned. She would provide him with the support she suspected he needed, and afterwards...

She pulled on some pale cotton jeans.

Afterwards she would make her exit from his life.

She would walk, before she was pushed.

CHAPTER ELEVEN

THE MANSION ROSE up before them. A monstrous monolith which dominated the land around and Leon could do nothing to prevent the shudder of distaste which ran down his spine. The last time he had seen this place he had been walking out with a rucksack and the predatory eyes of a frustrated woman burning into his back. Had Marnie detected the bitterness of his feelings and was it that which had prompted her to lay her fingers over his tensed biceps and to give it a soft squeeze? He swallowed. Did she realise what her touch could *do* to him? That sometimes she had the power to take some of the darkness away?

She was staring up at the multi-tiered concoction, her lips falling open as if she couldn't quite believe what she was seeing.

'This is your *home*?' she verified, but he shook his head in grim denial.

'This is where I grew up and lived until the age of sixteen,' he amended grimly. 'Do you like it?'

'Honestly?'

'Are you ever anything *but* honest, Marnie?'

He saw her swallow. 'I can't imagine ever living somewhere this big,' she whispered. 'It looks more like a museum.'

Leon rang the bell and waited but there was no welcoming committee to greet them. No sign of his father. Instead, the door was opened by a housekeeper—a stranger to him, obviously. Her hooded gaze ran over them both with calculating precision, her greeting more formal than warm.

'Kyrios Kanonidou has been making some last-minute adjustments before the ceremony and would like you to join him on the eastern terrace for a drink straight away,' she announced. 'If you would like to follow me, I will make sure your bags are taken up to your suite. Once your meeting with your father is finished, I will send one of the servants to accompany you there.'

Leon was about to inform the woman that he was in no need of any direction before reminding himself that he was here as a guest,

not to stamp his mark or assert his owner-
ship—which was non-existent anyway. And
nothing ever stayed the same, he reminded
himself—wasn't that apparent with every step
they took? As they walked through the wide
corridors, he became aware of how much had
changed.

The route was familiar, the décor was not.
Within its ornate elaborate shell, the building
had changed out of all recognition in the years
since Leon had last been here. All traces of
his childhood gone. It was as though he had
never been there—his presence wiped clean.
In some ways it felt liberating to acknowledge
this break with the past, but it still came as
a relief to step outside onto the sun-washed
tiles of the eastern terrace. Lush lemon trees
in pots adorned a space used mostly used for
breakfast and morning coffee and which was
currently deserted. A white balustrade framed
the dark blue sea and there were steps leading down to a beach of silvery white sand.

'Wow. What a view,' said Marnie, her long
blonde hair blowing lightly in the breeze.

He turned to look at her, remembering
the first time he'd met her. Looking defiant
and wounded as she lay on the sand—those
stormy eyes and killer curves luring him into

the most memorable sexual encounter of his life. Whoever would have thought that one day he would bring her here and she would stand overlooking the beach from where he used to take his morning swim? He realised how uniquely comfortable he felt in her company. 'You're ready to meet my father?'

'I think so,' she said, smoothing down her skirt. 'Is he *very* intimidating?'

'I'll leave you to judge for yourself,' said Leon, because suddenly Stavros was bearing down on them, sweeping onto the terrace accompanied by a small retinue of servants carrying trays covered with drinks and canapés. It had been a year since he'd last seen his father and, although he was definitely a little frailer, his posture was as upright as ever, resplendent in a fine wedding suit of silver-grey, a waxy white flower in his buttonhole. But Leon noticed as if for the first time how excess rather than age had carved out the deep ravines which made his features seem more ravaged than he remembered, and how the once-handsome face was now a pastiche of what it had once been. An unmistakable coldness flickered through his faded eyes as turned to survey his son, though Leon noticed how quickly he hid his reaction behind a pasted-on smile.

'Leonidas! I was worried you might not make it in time,' Stavros observed in perfect English as he made his way towards them.

'I said I would be here—and here I am,' replied Leon steadily. 'I'd like you to meet Marnie. Marnie Porter. You remember, I told you about her?'

'Ah, yes. The hairdresser.' The octogenarian's eyes narrowed. 'I understand we missed your company at dinner last night because of your dedication to your job, Miss Porter? I am in awe of such a work ethic. My son must be, too—for I have never been permitted to meet any of his girlfriends before!'

There was no doubt that Stavros was being mischievous and Leon wondered how Marnie would react to his teasing. But she seemed in no need of token reassurance, her familiar determination emerging as a gritty smile as she shook hands with his father. 'I'm delighted to meet you, Kyrios Kanonidou. Thank you for inviting me to your beautiful home,' she said firmly. 'I'm sure you must have plenty to talk about with your son, so I'll leave you to it.' Diplomatically, she walked across the terrace to gaze out at sea, leaving the two men alone to converse.

Leon didn't know what he had been expecting from this particular reunion, but it wasn't the unedifying discussion which followed. At times his father seemed almost...*jittery*, while at others almost borderline aggressive as he spoke to his son in voluble Greek. Leon wondered if the reality of marriage to a woman so young was losing some of its allure as the wedding approached—if perhaps his child bride was more demanding than Stavros had anticipated. Was history going to cruelly repeat itself by giving him another predatory wife with a wandering eye? As the conversation ended, Leon was aware that the vague suspicion with which he had initially viewed this wedding invitation had been eclipsed by a quiet and simmering anger.

He saw Marnie's eyes fixed on him as his father swept away with his entourage and as she came towards him he wished they could leave now. Board the luxury yacht which was moored and waiting in the marina in Phoinikas to take them to his house on the Thessaloniki coast. And although nothing was stopping them other than a misplaced sense of filial duty, Leon had given his word he would attend the ceremony and therefore he would do it, even if it was with gritted teeth.

'So. How did that go?' she questioned.

'If you don't mind, I'd rather not talk about it at the moment.' His words were clipped and he saw from her reaction that she had interpreted this as a put-down, but the reality was that a manservant had appeared to take them to their suite and, once there, Marnie realised she had very little time to get changed.

His own dressing swiftly completed, Leon walked over to the window while he waited for her, and stared outside, but the sight which greeted him did little to quell the tide of cynicism rising up inside him. Below, against the glittering backdrop of the sea, stood a wedding arch with rows and rows of chairs before it. Long tables were covered with white drapery, their surfaces crowded with silver and crystal. On the other side of the terrace, a wooden dance floor had been erected with a small dais at the back—presumably to house the band. And there were flowers everywhere. He'd never seen so many flowers. There were even small posies sitting on each of the seats, presumably one for each of the guests, who he could see were starting to arrive in a flurry of finery.

Leon's eyes narrowed. His father had insisted this would be a small and discreet ceremony. It certainly didn't look that way from here.

He heard a sound behind him and the moment Marnie walked into the room all his disdain evaporated, a pulse thundering at his temple as he acknowledged her stunning transformation. She was wearing a simple full-length dress in a blue as vivid as the Grecian sky, which skimmed her luscious curves and emphasised the pale curtain of her hair. She looked young and firm and fresh and he felt the tug of something deep inside him. He didn't know what he had been expecting, but it certainly wasn't *this*…

Her gaze was searching his face, as if she were trying to gauge his reaction. 'I know this is slightly different,' she said nervously, smoothing her palms over the material.

'Turn around for me,' he instructed silkily. 'What happened to the red dress you were supposed to be wearing?'

Marnie nodded as she did as he asked, unable to allay her sudden rush of nerves and wondering if she'd been too headstrong in her choice as she faced him. 'You would have preferred me to wear that instead? Do you mind?'

'Are you crazy? Why would I mind? You look absolutely sensational, Marnie. You must know that.'

Did she? Marnie swallowed. She looked more like herself—that was for sure. Most of the clothes his fancy stylist had purchased were perfect, but the red dress had felt like a step too far. Despite his assurances that the outfits were modest it had seemed too clingy and too provocative and when she'd stared at herself in the mirror, her shocked breath had frozen in her throat—but she couldn't possibly tell Leon the reason why.

Imagine his face if she did.

Imagine the dilemma he would face as a result of her disclosure—if he realised why it should disturb her so much.

It makes me look like my mother.

She'd used some of the money she'd been saving for Pansy to nip out from the salon with Hayley the following lunchtime to buy something different. Something more suited to a hairdresser's salary—although Hayley had persuaded her to be a bit more daring than usual. But at least now she didn't look a rich man's mistress, because that wasn't how she wanted Leon to remember her. Hadn't she already decided this wedding was going to be their swansong and she was going to make a graceful exit from his life when they arrived back in London? Her mouth dried. Even though the thought of leaving him was making her heart want to shatter into a million pieces...

'What's wrong?' he demanded. 'Your face has gone as pale as milk. What is it that you say in England—as if someone had walked over your grave?'

The pound of her heart felt like guilt and Marnie scrabbled around to come up with a reasonable explanation, because what would be the point of coming here if she was going to spoil the event with all her fears about the future? 'I guess meeting your dad was more nerve-racking than I'd anticipated and I'm wondering what on earth I'm going to say to the bride,' she babbled. 'You do realise she's younger than I am?'

'I think I've been quietly blocking out that fact,' he offered drily. 'Don't worry about it, Marnie. Just be yourself.'

She wondered how she could be 'herself' when she wasn't even sure she knew who that person was any more. Beneath her dress, she was still wearing some of the lingerie Leon had bought—which probably cost more than an entire month's pay cheque. Yet if she was being brutally honest, didn't she *like* the sensation of fine silk sliding over her skin? Sometimes she wondered what it was going to be like returning to 'normal' life when their affair was over—if she was going to find it a sobering comedown.

But her reservations were forgotten as he pulled her into his arms to graze his mouth over hers in a teasing kind of kiss. As his fingertips skimmed over her bottom, Marnie felt the inevitable ripple of desire and Leon must have felt it too because his hold on her tightened, his palms pressing against her buttocks.

'*Neh.* You and me both,' he murmured complicitly, his breath fanning her mouth. 'If you must know, I'd like to fast-forward the next few hours because I can think of some far more enjoyable ways of spending a weekend in Greece.'

'You want to go and visit some crumbling temples?' she questioned innocently.

'I want to take your panties off as quickly as possible but that will have to wait until later. Come on. Let's go.'

He laced her fingers with his as they

began to make their way through the maze-like property—and if Marnie was surprised at this unusually tactile display, she guessed it was because there was nobody around to see them. As they passed beneath elaborately painted ceilings and tall columns which emphasised the dizzying scale of the house, the touch of his skin felt electric. She told herself it didn't mean anything—even if she was discovering how much she liked this languid gesture of possession which marked her out as Leon's woman.

Which she wasn't.

Get real, she reminded herself fiercely. *That would imply some measure of permanence which has never been up for grabs. Your position in his life is short-lived and temporary.*

And very soon it was going to be over.

And the moment they stepped outside, everything changed. An instant buzz zipped around the grounds as people spotted them and started to converge on them, or rather—on Leon. When he let go of her hand Marnie felt as though she'd lost her anchor. This was way more than *a handful of guests*, she thought desperately. She was completely alone in a bobbing sea of bodies but she forced herself to smile brightly and to nod as if she understood, even though everyone was speaking in Greek.

Suddenly Leon was back by her side, a glitter of fury icing his blue eyes as he touched his fingertips to her waist. 'This place is like a damned circus,' he hissed. 'I feel like leaving right now.'

'We can't go yet. Come on, let's go and sit down.'

The scent of the flowers was so strong it was cloying and as they walked towards their seats Marnie could see heads turning to watch them. Was that because Leon was just so outrageously handsome, with the sunlight turning his skin to bronze and making his eyes look bluer than the nearby sea? Or were they wondering why he'd brought this unknown woman from England as his guest, instead of leaving himself free to chat up one of the many gorgeous women here?

As they sat down a sudden silence descended on the congregation and, along with everyone else, Marnie turned to see Stavros standing in the doorway of the enormous mansion. To the sound of loud cheers, he began to almost *sprint* towards the wedding arch and Marnie couldn't help thinking how sad it was. It was such an inappropriate speed for someone to make their way up the aisle and supposedly designed to imply that, despite his great age, he was still very fit.

The bride was fashionably late, her eye-popping figure revealed by a dress designed to do just that. The white satin gown was backless, plunging and split to the thigh—caressing every gym-honed curve of her incredible body. Despite her startling youth, she appeared to have had some work done on her face—either that or she'd had an allergic reaction to her lipstick.

Marnie had been to several weddings of questionable taste in her time, but surely you'd have to travel a long way to find one as awful as this. Her heart went out to Leon as his father kissed his new wife for much longer than was necessary. A man with waist-length hair who had been eyeing up the bride throughout the ceremony perched himself on a stool and started to croon a song to the newly-weds, even though he was obviously tone deaf.

And then, mercifully, it was over. Clouds of rose petals fluttered in the air as the couple turned towards the congregation and began to walk, arm in arm. Music began to be played—thankfully by some excellent bazooka players—and glasses of champagne were offered around.

But beside her Leon stood tense and unmoving, and as Marnie glanced up into his stony features, another feeling of concern flickered over her. 'Are you okay?'

His smile was edged with grit. 'It wasn't the most palatable occasion of my life, but at least it's over. I think we should have something to drink to celebrate that fact, don't you?'

He handed her a goblet of champagne but it tasted vinegary and Marnie surreptitiously tipped it into a nearby plant pot while nobody was looking. But Leon was looking. She glanced up to find his gaze fixed on her and suddenly she was transported back to those times when the foster home insisted on giving her macaroni cheese and standing over her while she ate it, even though they knew it made her retch. Once she'd been caught hiding the cold lump of food in her handkerchief and the red marks on her knuckles from the resulting caning had taken days to disappear. She shifted uncomfortably on her high heels.

'I didn't mean to—'

'Don't worry about it.' A wry smiled

touched the edges of his lips. 'It's fine. I agree. The champagne leaves a lot to be desired. I wonder if my new stepmother had a hand in choosing it—she doesn't exactly look like a woman of taste, does she?'

She followed the direction of his gaze to see that the newlyweds had taken to the floor for the first dance and the bride was strutting her stuff—seemingly oblivious to the presence of her new husband, who was jigging awkwardly by her side. It was excruciating to watch, but when the music came to an end and other couples started taking to the floor, Leon took the empty glass from Marnie's suddenly nerveless fingers and put it down.

'Come on, Marnie,' he said. 'Dance with me.'

Marnie glanced up at his stony features as they found a deserted space on the dance floor, thinking that there was a new brittleness about him all of a sudden. A sombreness which seemed to have settled over him like a dark mantle. She thought about the way his face had hardened when he'd been talking to his father on the terrace and she asked him again.

'What did Stavros say to you back there?'

There was a pause before he answered. A pause which went on for so long that she wondered if he'd heard her question, or whether he was just blanking it. And when he began to speak, his words were edged with iron.

'He thanked me for coming. He said it was important to him because it enhanced his reputation as a father, as well as giving my tacit seal of approval to the marriage. He also said he was pleased I'd done so well for myself, because all his money would be going to his new wife and her large and apparently impoverished family. Oh, and to my two stepbrothers, who have never done a day's work in their lives.'

'Oh, Leon.'

He shook his head. 'I don't want your pity, Marnie,' he said softly. 'Just like I don't want his damned money. I never did. That much hasn't changed. I'm just not sure why he made such a damned fuss about me coming here, if all he wanted to do was to inform me of the terms of his will.'

She hesitated. 'Maybe you being here means more to him than he's letting on and he's just being clumsy about expressing it.'

'Please don't go getting all sentimental on me.'

'I can assure you I'm the last person who could ever be accused of being sentimental.'

But as his arms tightened around her waist, Marnie realised that maybe some of her old ideas *did* need revisiting. It was weird. She'd always been envious of people who hadn't been poor, or who'd had a permanent home when they were growing up. And even more envious of those kids with parents, even if they weren't happy—because at least divorced or separated parents were *around*. But Leon had described the atmosphere in this place as toxic and not much had changed. It seemed there was to be no fairy-tale ending. Even now, after all these years.

And hadn't she wanted that to happen? Deep down, hadn't she hoped that Leon's icy heart might melt a bit, if he was successfully reunited with his father? And then what? That he'd suddenly realise he wanted more from their relationship than he'd previously imagined? Well, more fool her. Hope really *did* spring eternal.

She almost wished they weren't dancing because it felt so poignant as she realised this was probably the first and last time they would ever dance like this. As they moved in time to the music, she could feel the strength radiating from his powerful body as he pulled her closer, even though from the corner of her eye she could see people watching them. Too many people, she thought fleetingly before another wave of physical reaction blotted out her reservations. She thought how perfectly their bodies fitted together, despite the fact that he was so tall and she was so short. As if they had been designed to match like this.

Her heart contracted. She was going to miss him. More than she could ever say. How long would it take to forget a man who was so unforgettable? She realised how naïve she had been in believing that having Leon teach her about sex might help in any future new relationship. How was that ever going to be possible when the thought of being in another man's arms made her feel sick?

'Do you want…do you want to go and circulate?' she whispered, because now the dance was beginning to feel dangerously erotic. Her breasts were throbbing and tender and her skin was on fire. She could feel a silken tug at the juncture of her thighs as he tightened his hold on her and she swayed in his arms.

'No, Marnie.' His voice was uneven. 'The only thing I want to circulate is you.'

But that wasn't strictly true. Leon felt so turned on by having her in his arms like this that he could barely move. Against the musculature of his body her light weight and soft curves were tantalising, her subtle scent causing his heart to race like a train. With the tips of his fingers he began stroking her back, unable to resist touching her. He felt her instant shiver in response. He swallowed. It felt as though he were touching her bare skin and the provocation of that was making him grow hard. He thought her breasts seemed bigger than usual, as if they had expanded in the warmth of the Greek day. Or maybe the bodice of her dress could no longer defy gravity and contain their lush weight. He could feel her nipples getting tauter against his chest— and he buried his face in her hair, overcome by a sudden sensation which made him feel almost light-headed.

She was so different from any other woman he'd ever met and suddenly he found himself listing all the reasons why. She wasn't *pretending* to feel things in order to impress him. She didn't want his money and worked hard to pay her own way. She was here because she wanted to be and not because she wanted to be *seen* with him—indeed hadn't she been noticeably uncomfortable when she'd seen the crush of people when they'd arrived? His billionaire status meant nothing to her—she had proved that over and over again. Was it possible that this woman—the most unlikely candidate of all—should make him rethink what he wanted from life?

'Marnie,' he said huskily.

'Mmm?' She dragged her head away from where it had been resting against his chest and looked up into his face.

Her eyes were wide and her lips utterly irresistible and something clenched deep inside his chest. Oblivious to the watching eyes and his usual restraint in public, he started to kiss her. And suddenly the world tipped on its axis. He could feel the tremble of her lips and heard the sigh of pleasure she gave as his tongue began to explore her mouth. Or was he confusing that sound with his own shuddered groan, as he revelled in the taste of her and found himself thinking that he'd never known anything quite so delicious as this kiss.

He knew he should stop what they were doing and move this upstairs to the bedroom, but for once his famously steely self-control was eluding him. What the hell did she *do* to him, that all his certainties suddenly seemed as insubstantial as dust? He was fired up by something he'd never felt before, something he couldn't seem to evaluate. It was a feeling of excitement, tempered with calm. It was comfort and joy. It was anticipation and serenity—all spiced with a powerful sense of desire which pulsed through his veins like a fever. It was feeling as if he'd come home at last. Properly home. Not to a vast, cold mansion where he'd spent so much time alone, nor to any number of lonely luxury houses in enviable locations, but to a place of sanctuary which wasn't defined by bricks and mortar but by the soft, giving woman he was holding.

He kissed her again. And again. And perhaps if he hadn't been so captivated by her, he might have noticed the dark-clad figure moving stealthily around the edge of the dance floor. But he didn't. He didn't notice anything except the shining blonde in his arms.

CHAPTER TWELVE

IT WAS A NIGHTMARE.

It couldn't be happening.

But it was. It was happening right now and right here.

Marnie's first clue that something was wrong was an early-morning phone check to discover dozens of missed calls from numbers she didn't recognise, including several from Pansy, who *never* called at this time in the morning.

Sitting bolt upright in bed, she raked her hair out of her eyes and stared down at the screen, but even in the midst of such unusual telephone activity her thoughts were flitting elsewhere and there was no mystery about who was dominating them.

Leon.

She puffed out a sigh of sheer pleasure. He had taken his jet to Paris at some unearthly hour and she must have fallen asleep after he'd gone, but not before he'd kissed her with a hard stamp of possession which had made her toes curl. Her finger hovering above the call button, she couldn't prevent a smile of satisfaction from creeping over her lips.

They'd only arrived back from Greece late last night, leaving his father's house straight after the wedding—thank goodness—and then taking a yacht down to Leon's new property in Thessaloniki. And she had loved it. Just loved it. Its spectacular position on the edge of the sea was the only thing the house had in common with Leon's forbidding childhood home. With light-filled and airy rooms, it had been the antithesis of the cold mansion they'd just left.

In the warm October sunshine, they had picnicked on the beach and swum in the sea. Marnie had sailed for the first time in her life and surprised herself by enjoying it, although Leon was an excellent and very patient teacher. They'd even had a midnight skinny dip in his enormous infinity pool, with a giant moon reflected silver in the rippling waters. And they'd been having sex. Non-stop sex, actually.

Marnie leaned back against the pillows and

stared dreamily at the ceiling. At times, she'd thought Leon had been almost…

Loving?

No. Surely that was nothing but wishful thinking. But he had definitely been behaving differently towards her. For a start, he had practically ravished her on the dance floor at the wedding—something she *hadn't* been expecting. And it hadn't stopped there. It was difficult to put it into words, exactly, but his behaviour had made her decide that maybe she didn't need to walk away from the relationship quite yet. As long as she kept her emotions in check—and surely she'd had enough practice to be able to do *that*?—and they continued to be discreet now they were back in England, there was no reason why this blissful state of affairs shouldn't continue for a little while longer.

She stared at her phone but before she'd a chance to hit the call button an icon of a pouting Pansy began flashing on the screen and Marnie answered immediately.

'Morning,' she said cheerfully.

'Have you seen the online edition of the *Daily View*?' demanded her twin, without bothering to return her greeting.

'You know I never read the tabloids.'

'Well, maybe you should. In fact, I would study that one with particular care. And then you'd better call me back. And just to let you know—one of the stylists from Hair Heaven has put a link to the piece on social media and it's already had hundreds of "likes".' There was a short, tense pause. 'Oh, Marnie, what *have* you got yourself into? I knew getting yourself mixed up with Leon Kanonidou was only ever going to end in tears. Have you told him?'

'Told him *what*?'

'About mum.'

There was a pause as a trickle of fear started sliding down Marnie's spine. 'No,' she whispered. 'No, I've never told him.'

'Why *not*? When are you going to get it into your thick head that it's not your fault, Marnie?'

'He doesn't need to know,' she answered, her voice hollow.

Pansy gave a laugh which sounded bitter. 'Well, good luck with that. I think he's about to find out—if he doesn't know already.'

Now in a state of terror, Pansy cut the call and went straight into the sitting room to find her laptop. Plonking herself down on the sofa, she scrolled to the free, online version of the

Daily View newspaper, which apparently had one of the biggest circulations on the planet.

It didn't take long to find it—not when it was splashed all over the top of the page. Marnie's stomach twisted into a writhe of knots as she stared at it. Because there, in glorious Technicolor, was a photo of her dancing with Leon at his father's wedding. Only dancing didn't seem a very accurate way of describing what the camera had captured. They were all over each other. As if their bodies had been joined together with superglue. There were accompanying comments from some of the other guests saying how *close* they'd been, along with snatched photos which had obviously been taken on people's phones.

It was bad, but the headline made it even worse.

Upstaging his father's wedding!

Marnie's heart contracted as she read the piece.

When Greek shipping magnate Stavros Kanonidou (eighty-five) tied the knot with his latest young bride this week-

end, his billionaire son, Leonidas (thirty-three), made sure all eyes were focussed on him. It seems heart-throb Leon has exited the marriage market at last, judging by his tactile display on the dance floor with nubile blonde English hairdresser Marnie Porter.

Just who is Marnie Porter and how has she managed to land herself one of the world's most eligible bachelors?

Phone this number if you know. (We pay for any information used.)

Marnie felt faint. Dizzy. A wave of pain and regret made her glad she was sitting down because she honestly didn't think her trembling knees could have supported her. When her phone began to buzz, she looked down to see another unknown number flashing on the screen. A journalist? She didn't know and she didn't care. She turned it to silent just as Leon's chef tiptoed in to deposit a cup of steaming black coffee in front of her, but when she mimed eating—presumably asking if she wanted breakfast—Marnie shook her head because the thought of food made her want to heave.

But as well as the pain, the irony of the

situation didn't miss her. It seemed that just as she'd got used to this rarefied life with its servants and planes and luxury yachts it was about to be taken away from her. She didn't *care* about the trappings, the only thing she cared about was the man and she needed to speak to Leon. She badly needed to tell him before anyone else did.

He didn't answer. Not the first time she tried, nor even the fifth. After an hour had gone by, she sent him a text.

Please ring. It's urgent.

But Leon didn't ring, or text, and after she'd sent the chef away for the rest of the day Marnie began to pace around the huge apartment like a caged animal, staring out of the vast windows without really noticing the park's blazing autumnal display. It was past noon when she realised she hadn't even taken a shower and she was just emerging from the bathroom, wrapped in a towel, when she heard the sound of a key being turned in the lock.

She froze. And wasn't it funny the things which crossed your mind at moments of high tension? So that instead of wondering just how she was going to tell him, she found herself wondering whether or not she should call his name and let him know where she was.

But it seemed there was no need, because she could hear Leon striding down the corridor and when he walked into the bedroom, loosening his tie, she couldn't seem to read anything from the tight, closed look on his face. His icy gaze scanned over her and she thought about how he'd made amazing love to her that very morning and somehow she couldn't imagine that ever happening again.

'Get dressed and then come to my office,' he ordered succinctly. 'I'll be waiting.'

Here came another stupid dilemma—deciding what to wear. And although there were plenty of exquisite clothes in the wardrobe which Leon had bought for her, Marnie couldn't bring herself to put any of them on. The clock had struck midnight. It was time to return to her familiar rags. Wriggling into a pair of tracksuit bottoms, she swathed her bosom in a roomy top, unable to miss the faintly contemptuous curve of his lips as she walked into his office, where he was sitting perched on the edge of his desk.

'Sit down,' he said, gesturing towards the brown leather sofa on which they'd once spent a very passionate couple of hours one rainy Sunday afternoon.

'I'll stand if you don't mind,' she declined stiffly. As a doyenne of the formal reprimand, she was conscious that he might be employing a touch of psychological warfare here. Did he want her passively seated—and was he intending to make it seem as if he were interviewing her, as if she were his subordinate?

And aren't you?

Aren't you?

Had she ever imagined for more than a second that she was really his equal?

There was silence for a moment while he studied a paperweight containing an iridescent shell, before lifting his gaze to hers— and it seemed she had forgotten how beautiful his eyes were and how sometimes his gaze could wash over you, as brilliant and as blue as the ocean itself.

'So, where do we begin, Marnie?' he questioned heavily.

'That's up to you,' she answered, in a low voice. 'How much do you know? Have you been told that my mother was a prostitute?'

'Yes.'

She nodded. Had one of the journalists prised out that particular nugget and presented it to him, or had someone in his office been tasked with uncovering her past? It didn't matter. She had often wondered how it would feel to talk about this to someone, to open the door on a room which had been kept closed and locked for so long. And although she knew that what she was about to say was going to bring to an end this part of her life with Leon, wasn't there another part of her which felt a funny sense of relief to be able to unload the dark and heavy burden, after so many years of carrying it around?

'Do you want to hear why?'

'Not really.'

It hurt to think he didn't care enough to want to find out more—but wasn't that just another layer of hurt to add to all the others which were building up inside her?

'Well, I'm going to tell you anyway,' she said, suddenly fierce—and Marnie realised that maybe she *was* defending the indefensible. But really, she was defending her mum.

'She came from the north of England,' she said slowly. 'They said she'd had a tough childhood. A father who drank and who liked to beat her mother. He beat my mum, too, and I think…' For a moment her voice faded away as she recalled the other things she'd heard.

Things buried too deep ever to be resurrected. Dark things hinted at by social workers, too tired and overworked to know how to deal with two angry and confused little girls.

'Anyway, she ran away to London and got in with a bad crowd. It's as simple as that, really. There was no safety net—and if there was she had no idea how to access it. Nobody to look out for her. She got pregnant by one of her clients.' Her mouth was working like crazy now, but years of practice meant she was able to keep the prick of tears at bay. 'I guess I should be grateful that she kept us.'

She lifted her chin, aware that her voice was trembling, waiting for him to prompt her—and when he didn't, she continued of her own accord.

'I told you I didn't remember anything about my early years, but, of course, I did.'

'Yes,' he breathed. 'I imagine you did.'

'I remember we used to have to stay very quiet whenever she had clients round. I remember the sounds they used to make.' She pulled a face. 'That was probably what put me off sex for so long. We used to sit upstairs in our bedroom and I would whisper little games for Pansy to play to keep her amused. We always kept the door locked, of course. And it wasn't all bad. If…' Her voice wavered again. 'If mum had had a particularly good night, then she used to go to the corner shop next day and buy us a cake, for tea. Ch-cherry was our favourite.'

'Go on,' he said grimly.

Marnie nodded, but the bitter lump which had risen in her throat was suddenly making it very difficult for her to breathe. 'Then she got pneumonia. It was all very quick. One minute we were being taken into care while mum went into hospital and the next we were told she'd died.' She shrugged. 'And it was as if she had never existed.'

'You didn't go to the funeral?' he said, as though this mattered, as though he were remembering the secrecy surrounding his own mother's illness.

'No. Things were different then. As you know yourself. Apparently they thought we would get over the whole experience more quickly if we moved on. So we did. We were sent to a children's home and from there we were farmed out to various foster families, but nobody wanted to adopt us.'

'Why not?'

She shrugged. 'We were too damaged, I guess. Too suspicious and too close and too much of a handful. They tried to split us up but I made sure that was never going to happen.'

Marnie's knees felt wobbly and she would have loved to have taken Leon up on his offer and to have sunk into that squishy sofa, but that would mean she was looking up at him and would definitely put him at an advantage. And he certainly didn't need any more advantages. Besides, how would she be able to leave quickly and with dignity if she had to haul herself up? 'It's okay, Leon. You don't have to worry about how to tell me. It's over. I know that. Who wants a girlfriend with a past like mine?'

He stood up then and she could see the shadows which were flitting like dark clouds across his face, making him look like a Leon she didn't recognise. His blue eyes were boring into her with a coldness she'd never seen directed at her before.

'It's not okay,' he negated harshly. 'It might have been if you'd told me all this right from the start.'

'Really? And how would that have worked?' She gave a bitter laugh. 'Should I have thrown it into the conversation on our first date? Maybe confided it when I came to see you at your office, or murmured it as pillow talk a little further down the line? At what stage of our relationship should I have told you the truth, Leon?'

'But surely that's the whole damned point!' he ground out. '*That you didn't tell me the truth.* That you feigned ignorance and pretended. That in essence you *lied* to me, Marnie. And I can bear a lot of things, but not lies.'

Leon tugged off his tie and flung it to the ground as if it were choking him. And in a way, it was. Because her words had taken him hurtling right back to his own childhood. To the mother who had always appeared startled whenever he caught her taking tablets, explaining them away by saying she had a headache. A mother who told him she much preferred the shiny new wig to her own wispy hair—though he'd never really understood until afterwards why all those gloriously thick black locks had fallen out so suddenly. Not one honest answer had she given to any of his questions and he'd felt sidelined. As if he didn't count enough to be told the truth. As if he didn't matter. And that feeling had stayed with him, lying dormant inside him—always ready to rise to the surface if someone was deliberately dishonest.

'You didn't tell me the truth, Marnie,' he repeated quietly. 'And I'm afraid that's a deal-breaker for me.'

He saw all the colour leach from her face and thought the clipped finality of his final statement would be enough to send her running from the room, saving them face and saving them both from any more soul-bearing or heartache. And didn't he want that? Wouldn't that have made it—not easy— but easier for them both? But she didn't go. She just stood her ground like an immovable force. Dignified and proud, despite the sloppy clothes and her diminutive height, as she tilted a mulish face at him.

'And being used is a deal-breaker for *me*!' she hissed back.

Mutual mud-slinging was the last thing he wanted to engage in right now but he couldn't let her furious accusation pass. 'Being used?' he verified icily. 'And just how did I do that?'

'You used me to upstage your father on his wedding day!'

'You believe all that rubbish you read on the website?'

'Yes! Because that's what happened! I was

there, remember? You must have realised that everyone was watching you, because they'd been watching you from the moment we arrived. What better way to pay your father back than by stealing all his thunder? By showcasing your own youth and vitality in contrast with a man in his declining years?' She drew in a deep breath and he could see a tiny pulse hammering away at her temple, close to the moonlight sheen of her hair. 'You told me you were angry with him. Angry that he'd duped you into attending a wedding you secretly disapproved of, but you did it because you were hoping for some kind of closure and reconciliation, which he failed to provide. You don't want or need his fortune, but the fact that he's doling it out to other people must have hurt you more than you care to admit, because that's human nature.'

Her words faded away but Leon shook his head. 'You can't possibly stop now, Marnie,' he said grimly. 'Not when this is just starting to get interesting.'

She stared at him and he could see the hurt in her eyes, but was able to steel his heart against it because the slow pulse of anger in his blood was dominating everything.

'You didn't stop to think how all this might

impact on me, did you, Leon?' she questioned quietly. 'I mean, you were never demonstrative with me before, were you? You never so much as held my hand or kissed me in public and I was okay with that because I sensed that was the sort of man you were. Yet suddenly, you're all over me. I couldn't believe the way you were acting on the dance floor.'

He gave a short laugh. 'Neither could I.'

'So why do it?'

It was a question he wished she hadn't asked. A question he was under no obligation to answer. But he was aware that he couldn't chastise her for refusing to tell the truth and then do the same thing himself. 'Because I was going to suggest taking our relationship to the next level,' he said, his words deliberately flat, as if that would take the emotional sting out of them. 'I thought I was in love with you.'

Surely that was the key in getting her to leave. The deliberate use of the past tense, indicating he felt that way no longer. Surely she would be too proud to want him to witness the tears which were currently filling her beautiful grey eyes. But no. It seemed he had underestimated her tenacity, for she drew her shoulders back as if she were squaring up to him in a boxing ring.

'Ah, so *now* I understand,' she said. 'You didn't want to fall in love, did you? Not with me and not with anyone. You told me that right from the start. But emotions are messy things, aren't they, Leon? Sometimes they creep up on you when you're least expecting them. So I imagine finding out about my hidden past must have come as a huge relief to you. It gave you all the ammunition you needed to shoot our relationship down in flames. You could classify my behaviour as an abuse of trust when the reality is that it presented you with a handy get-out clause from having to commit.'

She sucked in a shuddering breath. 'And you want to know something, Leon?' she continued. 'I understand. In a way, I almost expected it. I mean, who would ever want to get involved with a woman like me? I know I'm not good enough. Don't you think I've always known that? But please don't make out that I'm the only one of us who resorted to subterfuge when it suited them!'

'Marnie—'

'No!' She dabbed a furious fist against each wet eye before fixing him with a glare.

'You make a big deal about me keeping parts of my life secret, but didn't you do exactly the same when we first met? Pretending to be some boho biker, rather than a billionaire tycoon?'

'You know why I did that,' he growled.

'I know what you told me. That you didn't want people muscling in on you and knowing how rich you are and that's why you keep a beaten-up old car in every place where you have a home. You had your reasons, Leon, just like I had mine. Do you really think yours are somehow more valid because you're so powerful?'

'You're twisting this, Marnie.'

'No. I'm telling you how I feel, but it's done now. Don't worry. I get it. It's over. It should never really have begun. And I'm out of here.'

She moved towards the door and instantly he slid from the desk. 'Where are you going?'

'That's none of your business.'

'It *is* my business if you're being hounded by journalists because of your association with me.'

'But I live in Acton and nobody knows that.' She gave a laugh which was edged with hysteria. 'Because I *am* a nobody!'

'Don't be so naïve, Marnie,' he snapped.

'Finding out where you live will be a piece of cake and if you try to use public transport you'll be a target. My driver will take you anywhere you need to go. If you like, I can send someone from my security team to keep their eye on you. And I'll leave a credit card on the side. Use it for whatever you need.'

She shook her head in disbelief. 'Have you even listened to a word I've been saying?' she demanded. 'Do you think that's the answer to everything—that you can just buy your way out of things, when the going gets tough? I don't want your damned money, Leon, and I don't want your damned driver—or your security team!'

And Leon was left with nothing but the sound of loud slamming as she stormed her way out of his office.

CHAPTER THIRTEEN

IT WAS ACTUALLY quite easy to 'disappear'.

Marnie realised she'd spent most of her working life influenced by the faint fear of not knowing what the future held. She'd been saving for that mythical rainy day for a very long time, which meant she'd accumulated quite a lot of cash which she could now use.

Because that rainy day had arrived.

Accompanied by her sister, she had left London—sneaking away as dawn was breaking over the city, with Pansy driving a borrowed and rather fancy car, although refusing to say whose car it was—'I'll tell you later…'

Hair Heaven had told her to take as much time as she needed and, at very short notice, Marnie had found a tiny cottage to rent on the edge of the Yorkshire Moors—chosen mostly because it reminded her of one of her favourite books from childhood and seemed to fit with the bleak mood she was trying to hide from her sister.

'It's good to be able to help you for a change,' Pansy said, once they'd managed to push open the rather stiff front door and she'd placed a steaming mug of tea in front of Marnie, as though she were recovering from some kind of sickness.

Which in a way, Marnie guessed, she was. There was obviously a reason why the expression *lovesick* had come about—and she was certainly portraying all the symptoms of it. She couldn't eat. Couldn't sleep. Couldn't stop thinking about the man who had stolen her heart and left her wondering how she was ever going to get it back.

Pansy waved a packet of chocolate biscuits in front of her but Marnie shook her head. 'I won't, thanks.'

'You should. You're looking peaky,' said Pansy disapprovingly.

'Unlike you,' said Marnie, eyeing her sister.

It was true. Pansy was positively glowing and had toned down the sequins and too-tight tops. She'd also had her hair cut so that it swung in a sleek blonde bob around her shoulders, instead of falling to just above her bottom in that retro hippie style. 'Why didn't you ask me to cut your hair for you?' she added suspiciously.

'You were too busy jetting off in private planes, weren't you?'

A lump rose in Marnie's throat and, quickly, she changed the subject. 'Whatever you're doing, just keep doing it. You look fantastic,' she said huskily.

The biscuit she'd been just about to munch into forgotten, Pansy smiled—a soft, sweet smile edged with contentment. Marnie had never seen her sister look like that before and suddenly the penny dropped, and she wondered what had taken her so long to work it out. 'You're in love?' she asked.

Pansy nodded. 'I am. I've been seeing Walker. Quite a lot, actually.'

'The barrister who defended you?'

'That's right.'

A flare of anxiety washed through her. 'Pansy, is that even *legal*?'

Her twin shot her a reproving look. 'Of course it is. It happens all the time, lawyers falling in love with their clients—although apparently it's always best to wait until the case is over.' She grinned. 'And Walker is way too ambitious to ever risk breaking the law.'

'And he doesn't mind—'

'That my mum was on the game and that I spent time in prison myself?' Pansy sighed and shrugged her shoulders. 'Well, obviously it's not the perfect CV for a barrister's wife but he says those experiences are what made me the woman I am today, and he loves that woman. Anyway, isn't the whole point of life supposed to be about learning from our mistakes and other people's? About redemption?'

'I'm sure it is,' said Marnie gruffly, knowing she had to get her twin out of here because any minute now she was going to break down and cry. 'Anyway, you'd better get back to him.'

'Marnie—'

'No. Honestly. I really don't want to hear it.'

'But you don't know what I was going to say.'

'Yes, I do. We're twins, Pan, and sometimes I know what you're thinking, though that's going to happen less and less, the closer you get to Walker. And that's the way it should be. I'm so happy for you. Really, I am. I think it's a wonderful love story, but I don't want to talk about Leon. Not now and not ever. I just don't. It…it hurts too much.' She drew in a deep breath, aware of just how much vulnerability she was revealing to her younger sister. And that was a first. 'Do you understand?'

Pressing her lips together as if she too was trying not to cry, Pansy nodded. 'I understand perfectly,' she whispered, and suddenly the two sisters were embracing, more tightly than they'd done in years. 'Just keep in touch, won't you?'

'Try stopping me,' answered Marnie fiercely, but once her twin had driven away in Walker's strangely silent electric car, she didn't have to pretend any more. For a while, she sat on an overstuffed armchair, buried her face in her hands and wept. She wept as tears trickled out from between her fingers and dripped onto her jeans. Until she felt exhausted, but in a way washed clean. And lighter, somehow—although the terrible ache in her heart hadn't gone away.

But as the next few days passed, Marnie tried to come to terms with what had happened, convincing herself that it was nothing more than she had ever expected. Like Pansy said, it was always going to end in tears. She couldn't allow what had happened with Leon to define her life in a negative way, she just couldn't. She needed to extract all the lovely elements they'd shared and remind herself that she was capable of a lot more things than she'd previously imagined. Of love, for a start—and how could any experience which had given her that ever be described as bad? It wasn't as if she'd ever *seriously* considered a future with him, was it? She'd get over it eventually, because people did. Every day thousands of people were getting their hearts broken and picking themselves up and carrying on.

Well, so would she.

Leon had managed to do it. Obviously. He hadn't tried to reach out and connect with her since she'd stormed from his Kensington apartment, had he? And she told herself she was glad about that. It would have been torture to speak to him, or see him and pretend that her heart wasn't shattering into a million pieces. She might have announced that her love for *him* was in the past tense but that wasn't true, was it? Love didn't disappear overnight, more was the pity.

Each day she would pull on some wellington boots, a waterproof coat and wide-brimmed hat and set off across the green-grey landscape of the brooding moorland, her stride lengthening as she got further away from the cottage. She'd bought herself an ordnance survey map and had started to explore the area in detail. It was so beautiful out here—in a very stark and elemental way. There were rocks and waterfalls and circling birds of prey. She was completely alone and yet somehow that felt okay.

One afternoon she had a slight wobble on her way back to the cottage, when she thought she spotted a man on the horizon, surveying the landscape through a pair of binoculars which glinted in the winter sun. The tall and brooding figure so reminded her of Leon that her heart constricted very painfully and tears sprang to her eyes. But thankfully the sound of a bird distracted her and when she turned back again, the man had gone. And that was normal too. *You're not going mad at all,* she reassured herself. It was probably a common phenomenon to imagine you'd seen someone when you'd been thinking about them as obsessively as she had about Leon Kanonidou.

She was tired when she let herself back into the cottage, but it was a very satisfying sort of tiredness. It wasn't like working out at the gym but a much more gratifying form of exercise, she decided. Peering into the tiny mirror over the bathroom sink, she appeared to have lost some of the haunted look which had made her face look so sallow recently and she wondered if it was time to leave London for good. Perhaps she should make the break from Hair Heaven permanent. She could move to somewhere like Yorkshire and see if she could get the backing to set up a little salon of her own. It was good to make plans. It made the future seem less bleak.

It was growing dark and she was deciding which book she would start reading this evening, having told the cottage owner that she didn't mind not having any broadband—how stupid was that?—when she saw the flare of headlights on the approaching track and heard the purr of a car drawing up outside the cottage.

Her heart raced and she knew then that she hadn't *imagined* a man who looked like Leon on the Yorkshire Moors. Because no other man looked like Leon and no other man ever could. He was here. Somehow he had managed to track down where she was staying. On the other side of that door was the man she loved with all her heart.

And she didn't know if she could face him. Wouldn't it set her recovery back and prolong the torture if she allowed her eyes to feast on him once more?

The loud knock reinforced his identity as much as the powerful car he was driving. She'd heard a knock like that once before when she'd been in Greece, feeling miserable and foolish after losing her virginity to him and realising he wasn't the man she thought he was. But she was a different Marnie now. She might be badly hurt, but she had always been strong. The question was whether she was strong enough to cope with seeing him again.

He was probably expecting her to play push-pull. To act all coy while not quite managing to hide her excitement at the realisation that he'd driven all this way to see her. Telling him to go away while expecting him to kiss her into changing her mind. He probably thought she would allow him to seduce her in front of that stupid damp fire, which she had been trying unsuccessfully to light. Well, he could go to hell!

She walked over to the door and pulled it open, trying not to react to his dark and windswept beauty as, coolly, she met his gaze.

'Who do you think you are? Heathcliff?'

'I hope not.' His voice was wry. 'Because I haven't come here to see a ghost.'

'I can't believe you've read *Wuthering Heights*.'

'Why? Because I'm Greek, or because I'm a man?'

Suddenly her knees sagged. She mustn't allow herself to get distracted. She mustn't. She must not put herself in emotional danger. Because suddenly the idea that she possessed some kind of inner strength was in grave doubt. 'Why are you here, Leon?'

'You must know why I'm here.'

'I'm afraid I don't. I think I may have mentioned before that I'm a hairdresser, not a mind-reader.'

'I'd like to come in.'

She made a play of hesitating but she knew it was a lost cause. Because no way was she going to send him away without hearing what he had to say—he knew that and she knew that. But that didn't mean she had to take his coat, or offer him a drink, did it? Why was he here? she wondered caustically. Had he been warned that a journalist had contacted her last week, offering her an eye-watering amount of money if she agreed to cooperate on a profile piece about the enigmatic billionaire—and was he seriously worried that she might go ahead and do it?

She stared at him. 'So?' she questioned, as coldly as she could.

Leon nodded in response to her terse greeting but he didn't speak straight away, knowing he had to choose his words carefully because surely these were the most important words he would ever say. He could see she was still angry and hurt—and he couldn't blame her for that. Not for the first time, he recognised that the forgiveness he sought from Marnie Porter was by no means guaranteed and she might not *want* to forgive him. What if it was already too late—if she had decided that she was well rid of his privileged but strangely antiseptic life? He felt the thud of pain. Of dread. Of fear. And he wondered how he could have been so emotionally brutal with her.

'I thought a lot about what you said, Marnie.'

'Good. I hope you can learn from it. I hope we both can.'

'Marnie…' He shook his head in frustration, realising that he had wanted her to make it easy for him by guessing what was on his mind. That she would be able to detect his pain and begin the healing process by forgiving him. But she was right. She wasn't a mind-reader, nor should he expect her to be. And he couldn't escape from his feelings or from learning to express them, not if he wanted her.

'What you said—'

'I said a lot of things, Leon.'

'I know you did—but one of them stuck in my mind more than any of the others.'

She stared at him. 'About my mum?'

'No. Not at all. Nobody should be blamed for their parentage, because that's something over which we have no choice or control.' He raked his fingers back through his windswept hair. 'I'm talking about when you told me you weren't good enough.'

She shifted awkwardly and stared down at the flagstone floor. 'Oh, that.'

'Yes, that. Because that's the craziest thing I've ever heard. You protected your sister through the most difficult of circumstances, all through your childhood. You forged a career for yourself and you've stuck at it. You made your own way in the world and took less from me than anyone else I've ever met. You have suffered knock-backs and the sort of prejudice which would have felled most other people, but not you. And somehow, along the way, you made me realise I was capable of feeling stuff. Stuff I'd always run away from before. You're more than good enough by anyone's reckoning, but especially by mine.'

'Thanks,' she said woodenly, her head still bent.

'And I realised something else,' he said slowly. 'That maybe I deliberately failed to give you the opening to tell me about your mother before. There were plenty of times I could have asked you more, but I *liked* your reluctance to talk about the past. It seemed to offer a protection against the true intimacy I had spent my life trying to avoid. Do you understand what I'm trying to say to you, Marnie? That in a way, I condoned your secrecy.'

She shrugged. 'Sure.'

'I've missed you so much.' He swallowed. 'And the question I need to ask you now is whether you could forgive me?' he questioned unsteadily. 'Because I love you, Marnie Porter. I love you in a way I never believed I could love anyone and I can't imagine spending my life without you.'

She looked up then and, though her eyes were very bright, she was shaking her head, a blonde halo of hair shimmering in the lamp-light. 'I'm afraid that's not enough, Leon,' she said. 'The trust between us has been broken.'

'Then let's repair it.'

'I don't want to repair it.'

His heart was pounding—its loud thunder edged with fear. 'Why not?'

'Because...'

Her mouth was working and he could see her trying to keep a rein on her own emotions.

'Because I don't want to get hurt again,' she burst out. 'I've had a lot of trouble adjusting to life without you, but I'm managing and every day it's getting easier. If we start seeing one another again, then we run the risk of breaking up all over again and I couldn't bear it.' She sucked in a deep breath and looked him straight in the eye. 'I'm strong,' she added. 'But I really don't think I'm that strong.'

He wanted so much to hold her—to comfort and kiss her—but the flash of her eyes was very definitely telling him not to touch. 'What if I told you that I want to spend the rest of my life with you? That I want to marry you?' he said huskily. 'What if I told you that I've sold off two large divisions of my company, which means we can live wherever you want to live. Maybe Thessaloniki? If you'd like that,' he amended hastily.

'You've *sold* part of your company?'

'Sure.' He shrugged. 'I've been simplifying my life so that I could devote the next section of it to you—that's what's been keeping me busy. You haven't seen the news? It's been all over the internet.'

'I haven't got any internet here. And even if I had, I certainly wouldn't have been reading anything about *you*.'

Leon's heart was beating very fast as he realised that this woman needed a declaration of love so powerful that never again would she be in any doubt of his feelings for her. She'd said she didn't know if she had the strength to risk having a relationship with him again, but he knew she did. He just had to convince her of that.

'I love and admire you more than anyone I have ever met, Marnie,' he said slowly, and very deliberately. 'I love your pride and feistiness and your ability to make me laugh. I love waking up in the morning and finding you there beside me, so that I can kiss you. I like your company more than anyone else's and I like you lying next to me when I wake in the darkness of the night. And I find myself imagining…' For some reason, his voice had started to crack. 'Imagining you,' he breathed unevenly. 'With a baby at your breast. Our child. A child we would love and protect with all our hearts. A child we would be honest with. There will be no more secrets between us from now on, my love. *Agape mou.* Just a shared life together. Will you share that vision with me, Marnie—will you journey down that road with me?'

As she heard the emotion underpinning his words, Marnie could feel the tears welling up in her eyes as she looked up into his beloved face. At the bronzed beauty of his sculpted features and the mouth she had thought so hard and unforgiving the first time she'd ever seen him. But Leon had crafted himself a mask to present to the world, the same as she had, she realised. A mask intended to conceal the pain they'd both suffered—a pain which had made them keep people at arm's length.

Yet somehow the two of them had come together—and how. They had got it wrong the first time around but he was right, they could start again. Because that was what life was all about.

About hope. And redemption. And renewal.

And love. Most of all it was about love. A love she had never imagined could be hers.

'Yes,' she whispered. 'Yes, I will journey down that road with you. Because I love you too, with all my heart. I think I've loved you from the moment I first set eyes on you, Leon Kanonidou.'

'So you'll marry me?' he verified fiercely. 'As soon as possible?'

She smiled. 'Yes, I'll marry you. But will you please hold me now? Because more than anything, I badly need you to kiss me.'

As his arms went round her, she sank lovingly into his embrace, feeling his warmth and protection as the sheer joy of being reunited with him flooded through her body. With tender fingers he dried the tracks of her tears and brushed the awry hair away from her cheeks and he lowered his lips to hers in what felt like slow motion.

But it was worth the wait.

Oh, yes. Definitely worth the wait.

Because that one kiss healed their past and sealed their future and made them realise how glorious their shared present was.

In fact, it was safe to say that it was the best kiss of their lives.

EPILOGUE

MARNIE HAD JUST positioned the final fondant dinosaur on top of the cake when the sound of movement outside the window captured her attention. With sunlight glittering off the nearby sea, she glanced up to see Leon approaching and thought—as she always did—what perfect timing he had. A visual feast in sawn-off jeans and a black T-shirt, he was running to keep up with two sand-covered little boys. Their sons. Their twin sons. Their two beautiful boys who would be four years old tomorrow, and who brought their besotted parents unimaginable amounts of joy. She swallowed, overcome with emotion which was never far from the surface—particularly during the last few weeks.

Every day she gave thanks for her life and her marriage because it hadn't all been plain sailing. Conceived early in their marriage, and born seven weeks prematurely, Theo and Atlas had been terrifyingly tiny when they had been delivered in Athens. Their parents had kept a tense vigil on the neonatal unit and Marnie had been shocked by the waxen pallor of her husband's face and the bleak terror she could read in his eyes.

But those little boys had come battling through and today were as healthy and robust as any of their friends, five of whom would be joining them tomorrow for a raucous birthday picnic on the beach, along with their aunt and uncle. Pansy and Warren were flying in later on Leon's private jet, along with their russet-haired daughter, Bryony— who was a loveable little terror. Warren was now one of the most successful barristers in the country and Pansy had become a valued prison visitor in London. She was even on the lecture circuit, giving increasingly popular talks about the realities of women's experiences in jail. As she was fond of telling anyone who asked—nobody knew the inside of a cell as well as she did.

Marnie sighed. Who would ever have thought that fate could have done such a satisfying flip-flop and allowed the two Porter sisters to find true happiness?

'That was a very big sigh,' came a silken comment from behind her and Marnie felt a shiver of inevitable expectation rippling down her spine as she heard Leon's voice.

She turned round, her heart clenching with pleasure. His blue eyes were bright against the bronzed gleam of his skin, but these days his raven-dark hair was styled a little longer and looked *very* sexy. She cut it herself, of course. In fact, lots of his friends had asked if she would cut theirs, too, but Marnie had resisted. She had loved her time as a hairdresser but other things beckoned to her now. With the help of their beloved nanny, Christina, she took an inordinate amount of pleasure from being a mother. She was on the board of trustees of a children's home and, assisted by the philanthropic arm of Leon's pared-down business, she hoped she was helping to make a real difference in the lives of those children. In fact, next week a tiny orphaned baby girl they were fostering was coming to the newly decorated pink nursery upstairs, which had been prepared just for her. She bit her lip. Well, that had been the theory.

'It was a sigh of contentment,' she informed her husband as he slid his arms around her waist.

'But also one of faint concern,' he noted as he traced the tiny frown on her brow with the tip of one finger.

'Where are the boys?'

'Christina has insisted they remove all that sand in the bath and, afterwards, they've decided they want to make welcome cards to give to their new baby sister next week.'

She grinned. 'Aw. That's so sweet.'

'Mmm. And then they're going to "play" chess.'

Marnie grimaced. 'I hope they don't start fighting again.'

'Only time will tell.' He smiled. 'Which gave me the opportunity to come and find my beautiful wife, to admire the birthday cake she's made and to wonder why she's looking a little worried.'

He was so perceptive! Marnie touched her fingers to his shadowed jaw—treasuring a moment she'd prayed for but which she'd thought would be denied them for ever. Because even though the doctors had told her it was fine for her to have another baby, up until now it had never happened. She had convinced herself she was okay with that, and revelled in the fact that she had lots of blessings to count. Twin blessings, actually—as well as an adorable baby girl who was soon going to be joining their family. But now...

'I'm pregnant, Leon,' she whispered, watching the series of emotions which crossed the face of a man who no longer kept his feelings hidden away. She could see hope and fear and joy—all those things which most people felt every day of their lives. 'I'm... I'm having your baby,' she said, just in case it hadn't registered. 'Are you happy?'

Leon hoped his tight embrace reassured her on that point and as he pulled her closer he could hear the combined thunder of their hearts. *'Agape,'* he said shakily, coming to terms with what she had just told him before uttering a silent prayer of gratitude. Because he had never imagined life could be like this. With his loving wife and two amazing sons, they had created the perfect family. He had thought things couldn't get any better, but he had been wrong. But then, he had been wrong about so many things before he had met Marnie.

'Am I happy?' he echoed slowly. 'Let me tell you that my happiness is right off the scale.'

'But we're going to have *two* new babies in the house now! And four children in total.'

'Shh.' He kissed the tremble of her lips. 'We'll cope. We coped with our two boys, just as we will with little Athena and her new brother or sister. We have enough love between us for an army of children in our lives, Marnie. Surely you know that?'

She nodded, smiling through the tears he recognised as tears of joy. He thought of all the ways he could respond to her news. Later, he would take her to their room and pay homage to her with his body. He would spoil her and cherish her and insist she rested. But for now there was only one thing she needed to hear, which happened to be the only thing he wanted to say.

'I love you, Marnie. *Se agapo.* For the rest of my days, and beyond.'

Their kiss was slow and very passionate, interrupted only by a furious accusation from upstairs, shouted in perfect English.

'Atlas, you're *cheating*!'

* * * * *

Lost in the magic of
Secrets of Cinderella's Awakening?
You're sure to love these other stories
by Sharon Kendrick!

His Contract Christmas Bride
Cinderella in the Sicilian's World
The Sheikh's Royal Announcement
Cinderella's Christmas Secret
One Night Before the Royal Wedding

Available now!